THE CHRISTMAS BOOK

ENID BLYTON

THE CHRISTMAS BOOK

Illustrations by Gavin Rowe

A Piccolo Book

PAN BOOKS LTD
LONDON

First published 1944 by Macmillan and Co Ltd.
This edition published 1971 by Pan Books Ltd.,
33 Tothill Street, London, S.W.1.

ISBN 0 330 02873 1

2nd Printing 1972

*Made and printed in Great Britain by
Cox & Wyman Ltd, London, Reading and Fakenham*

CONTENTS

Foreword

There is no time of the year at which we honour old customs more than at Christmas-time. The whole season is full of them, and their beginnings go back down the centuries into the mists of time.

We keep many of these old customs without knowing their meaning – but it adds much more to their interest if we know how they began, where and why. Why is plum pudding called *plum* pudding, when there are no plums? Why do we always hang up holly and mistletoe? Why do we give presents, and have a Christmas tree? Who was Santa Claus?

This book tells the story of a family who like to keep Christmas properly, and in the course of the story, most of the old customs are explained in, I hope, an interesting and natural way, so that the child reader will learn and enjoy at one and the same time.

For a great deal of my information I am indebted to my good friend, Mr L. J. F. Brimble, who spent much time and trouble hunting for the origins and meanings of many of our curious old customs. This information I have moulded into the story. I should here like to take the chance of thanking him for his kind help, and of expressing my real gratitude.

ENID BLYTON

Christmas Holidays

Heap on more wood – the wind is chill;
But let it whistle as it will
We'll keep our Christmas merry still.

Walter Scott

'Hurrah! Christmas holidays at last!' said Susan, running
into the house joyfully. She was just back from boarding-
school with her brother Benny, who had broken up the same
day.

He came into the house behind her, carrying a heavy bag.
His mother was paying the taxi outside. Benny set down the
bag, and gave a yell.

'Ann! Peter! Where are you? We're back!'

Ann and Peter were the younger brother and sister still at
home. They came tearing down the stairs and flung themselves on Benny and Susan.

'Oh! Welcome back! You're earlier than we expected!
Do you know were going to the pantomime on Boxing Day?'

'Are there any Christmas cards for us?' said Susan. 'Have
any come yet? Ooooh – I do love Christmas-time.'

'Yes – the Christmas hols are the best of all,' said Benny,
going off to help his mother with more luggage. 'Presents –
and puddings – and stockings – and cards – and Christmas
trees – and pantomimes – it's a lovely time!'

'There are lots of cards already,' said Peter. 'We haven't
opened yours, Susan, or Benny's. And Mother's ordered a

'Hurrah! Christmas holidays at last!'

fine Christmas tree – and we've stirred the Christmas pudding, and wished. It's a pity you weren't here to wish too.'

'You haven't got any decorations up yet,' said Susan, looking round. 'I'm glad. I do so like to help with those. I don't like you to begin Christmas customs without me here. I like to share in them all.'

'That's why we waited!' said Ann, jumping up and down. 'We wanted you and Benny to share. What fun we shall have!'

The luggage was brought in and taken up to the children's bedrooms. Susan went once more into the room she shared with little Ann, and Benny ran into the one he shared with Peter. How good it was to be back home again – and with Christmas to look forward to.

The children unpacked, and Mother sorted out their clothes, some to be washed, some to be put away, some to be mended. They all talked at once at the tops of their voices.

Mother laughed. 'How any of you can hear what the others say when you don't stop talking for one moment, I can't think!' she said. 'But it's nice to hear you all. Benny, *what* has happened to this stocking? It doesn't seem to have any foot.'

'Benny won't hang *that* stocking up on Christmas Eve,' said Ann, with a little giggle.

'He won't hang his stocking up any more, surely?' said Mother. 'He's too big. After all, he's ten now.'

'Well, I'm going to, said Benny, firmly. 'I don't see why I shouldn't, just because I'm ten. It doesn't matter whether I believe in Santa Claus or not, I can still hang up my stocking, and I know it will be filled. So there, Mother!'

'All right, Benny, you hang it up,' said Mother, still

wondering how it was that Benny's stocking had no foot. 'It's nice to keep up these old Christmas customs. There are such a lot of them.'

'There are, aren't there?' said Susan. 'I wonder how they all began. Mother, why do we hang up our stockings – who first thought of that?'

'I really don't know,' said Mother.

'And why do we put up holly and mistletoe?' said Ann. 'Holly's so prickly – it's a silly thing to put up really, I think. And why do we kiss under the mistletoe?'

'Oh dear – I don't really know,' said Mother. 'These customs are so very very old – goodness knows how they began!'

'Well, I know how Christmas began,' said Ann. 'It's the birthday of the little Christ. Mother, are you going to tell us the Christmas story, as you always do, on Christmas Eve?'

'Would you like me to?' said Mother.

'Oh *yes*!' said all the children at once.

'Mother, that's one of *our* customs,' said Susan. 'It's not a very old one, not nearly as old as the customs we keep at Christmas-time – but it's a very nice family custom of ours, so we'll go on with it.'

'And we'll choose carols and sing them too,' said Ann. 'I like carols better than hymns – they are much merrier, aren't they?'

'Very well,' said Mother. 'We will keep up our little family custom this Christmas as usual – carols on Christmas Eve, and the Christmas story.'

'And then off to bed and to sleep, whilst Santa Claus comes down the chimney, very secretly and quietly, to leave his presents!' said Ann.

'It's funny he should hate to be seen giving his presents,'

said Peter. 'We are always supposed to be asleep when he comes. Mother, who was Santa Claus, really?'

'Well – I really don't know,' said Mother. 'What a lot of questions you ask me today. I keep saying "I don't know, I don't know." Do ask me a question I can answer now.'

'Well – why is Christmas pudding called *plum* pudding?' asked Benny, at once. 'There aren't any plums in it.'

'I don't know that either,' said Mother. 'I begin to think I am not at all clever.'

'And what is the Yule log?' said Susan. 'I am always hearing about Yule-tide and the Yule log, but I never know exactly what Yule means.'

'Neither do I, really, except that it is another name for Christmas-time. You'd better ask Daddy all these questions when he comes home. He is cleverer than I am.'

Now the trunks were unpacked, and were put up into the loft for four whole weeks. It was tea-time, and the children rushed downstairs to a lovely tea. Mother always had a special cake for the first day the children came home, and special biscuits.

'I love the first few hours at home,' said Susan. 'It's all so deliciously new and exciting – then it gradually gets nice and familiar and homey. Mother, when are we going to begin the decorating?'

'Tomorrow, if you like,' said Mother. 'Our holly trees in the garden are full of berries this year – and the farmer has said you may go to the big oak trees in his field and cut some mistletoe for yourselves, if you like.'

'But why should we go to the *oak* trees for mistletoe?' said Ann, in wonder. 'Doesn't mistletoe grow on its own bush or tree?'

The others shouted with laughter. 'There *isn't* a mistletoe tree,' said Benny. 'It only grows on other trees – oak trees, for instance, and apple trees.'

'How funny,' said Ann. 'I'd like to see it.'

'You shall, tomorrow,' said Mother. 'Benny shall take you to the farmer's field, and he can climb up and cut some mistletoe and throw it down for you.'

'We'll cut holly too, and bring stacks of it in,' said Susan. 'And we'll make some paper-chains, and get out the silver stars and bells we had last year, to hang down from the ceiling. Oh, we *shall* have fun!'

'And what about the ornaments for the Christmas tree?' said Benny. 'We'll get those too. I hope there won't be many broken, they're so pretty and shiny.'

'We'll find the big silver star that goes at the very top of the tree,' said Susan, 'and we'll get out the little old fairy doll and put her under it. Mother, isn't Christmas-time lovely?'

'It is,' said Mother. 'Well, you children will have plenty to do these few days before Christmas, if you are going to do the decorating of the house, the dressing of the Christmas tree, the sending of cards, and the buying of presents.'

'You'll be busy too, won't you, Mother?' said Ann. 'You said you must boil the pudding again – and make the Christmas cake – and buy some crackers for us – and finish making some of your presents.'

They finished their tea, and then they heard the sound of a key being put into the front door.

'It's Daddy!' cried Susan and Benny and rushed to welcome him.

'Well, well, you've grown again!' said Daddy, hugging them both. 'Have you got good school reports? Who's going to help with the decorating tomorrow? I've got the day off, so I can take you all out to get holly and mistletoe!'

'Oh, lovely!' cried Susan. 'Yes, we've got good reports. I'm top of my form. Oh, Daddy, it's lovely to be home for Christmas!'

'Yes – Christmas is a proper family time,' said Daddy, hanging up his hat. 'All the old customs to keep up, the old carols to sing, the old tales to tell!'

'Well, I hope you know a lot about the old customs, Dick,' said Mother, kissing him. 'These children have been pestering me with Christmas questions, and I can't seem to answer any of them. I feel so stupid.'

'I don't feel like a lot of questions tonight,' said Daddy. 'Tomorrow, perhaps.'

And with that promise they settled down again. They all felt very happy. They were home together, beneath one roof. It would soon be Christmas, the season of goodwill, good cheer, and kindness.

'Christ-mas,' said Susan, separating the two syllables. 'I suppose it means Mass of Christ. What does "mass" mean, in the word Christmas, Daddy?'

'Feast or holiday,' said Daddy. 'The Feast of Christ, a holiday in His honour. There is Michael-mas, too, and Candle-mas.'

'Christ-mas is the nicest time of all,' said Susan. 'People in olden times thought so too, didn't they, Daddy, and feasted and made holiday?'

'They certainly did,' said Daddy, 'but I am sure they were not happier than *we* shall be this Christmas-tide.'

Bringing Home the Holly

With holly and ivy,
So green and so gay,
We deck up our houses
As fresh as the day.

Robin's Almanac

The first day of the holidays was sunny and bright. Frost had come in the night, and the grass outside was white and crisp – good to walk on. The children looked out of the window, and longed to be out in the sun, cutting the gay holly.

'It's lovely that Daddy's got the day off today,' said Susan. 'He's such fun to be with and he's not like some fathers I know. He really talks to us!'

After breakfast they all put on hats and coats, and went out into the garden. Daddy, Benny, and Susan had sharp knives for cutting holly sprays. Peter and Ann were to set the cut sprays neatly together on the grass, ready for taking indoors. Then they would all help in putting them up.

'Now, you two take those thick tall bushes,' said Daddy to Benny and Susan. 'I'll have to get the ladder to go up this tree. I'll cut some beautiful sprays from it. Aren't the berries lovely and thick this year?'

'Yes – and what a lovely scarlet!' said Susan. 'Daddy, why do you put up holly at Christmas-time? Does holly mean holy tree?'

'Yes,' said Daddy. 'It's been used for so many, many years

as a decoration in our churches, you see. There are quite a number of legends about it. I'll tell you some when we have finishing cutting, and are having a bit of rest and a cup of cocoa at eleven o'clock. But I can't talk and cut holly at the same time.'

Daddy fetched the ladder and went up the tree. Soon big sprays of the prickly branches were falling to the ground, and Ann and Peter were kept very busy picking them up.

'They *are* spiney!' said Ann, in dismay. 'Look, this leaf has made my finger bleed, Peter.'

Peter looked. 'It's nothing,' he said. 'I say, Ann, that little drop of blood on your finger is just the colour of the holly berry, look!'

So it was, as brilliant a scarlet as the gleaming berries. Ann wiped away the blood, and went to fetch her gloves. Then she wouldn't feel the pricks so much.

Susan and Benny worked hard. Daddy had shown them how to cut out sprays from the very thickest part, so that they would not spoil the shape of the bushes.

Ann and Peter ran in and out of the house with the berried sprays. At eleven o'clock Mother came out with a tray. On it was an enormous jug of cocoa, and a plate of biscuits.

'Oooh, lovely!' said Ann. 'Where shall we have it?'

'In the summer-house,' said Susan. So the tray was taken there, for it was a nice day. Susan poured out the cocoa. Daddy climbed down his ladder, and came to join them. He had a bright spray of holly stuck into his coat.

'That's for the Christmas pudding,' he said. 'It's such a thickly berried little spray.'

'I like holly,' said Benny. 'Its leaves are so smooth and shiny, and the berries are so brilliant. Daddy, the birds don't

The Roman people used to hold a great fea

go for holly berries nearly as quickly as they go for other berries, do they?'

'No, they don't,' said Daddy. 'They are not so nice – and if *you* ate them, they would make you terribly sick.'

'Is the holly berry like a gooseberry?' said Ann, squeezing one.

'Open one and see,' said Daddy. 'They are not like them at all. They have four tiny "stones" inside, containing the seed.'

'So they have,' said Ann. 'Daddy, why are the leaves so spiney?'

'Well, you could think of that for yourself,' said Daddy. 'Spines or thorns are nearly always grown by plants to prevent themselves being eaten.'

nd they decked the temples with holly

'That holly tree you have been cutting has smooth-edged leaves right at its top,' said Susan. 'There are no spines at all on the top branches, Daddy.'

'Well, there is no fear of a cow or horse having a long enough neck to reach right up to the top!' said Daddy. 'So spines often don't grow on the leaves higher up. Now – what was it you were asking me before, about the holly?'

'You said you would tell us some old tales about the holly,' said Susan. 'Daddy, was holly first used as a decoration when Jesus was born?'

'Oh no,' said Daddy. 'Holly was used long before that. Years before, the Roman people used to hold a great feast at this time of year, the feast of their god Saturn, and they decked his temples with the holly, as well as with other ever-greens.'

'Why did they use evergreens?' asked Ann. 'Just because they were green?'

'People of olden times had a strange belief,' said Daddy. 'They thought, you see, that there were many gods and goddesses living in the woods and in the hills among the trees and bushes. Well, when the wintry weather came, they thought these gods would be cold. So they brought evergreen boughs into their houses and temples, thinking that the forest gods and goddesses would be able to come with them, and nestle in the greenery to escape the bitter frosts outside.'

'Oh,' said Benny, 'what a queer idea. Did the old folk long ago hang up sprays just as we do?'

'They often made them into long festoons,' said Daddy, 'and they sometimes used fruit leaves, flowers and grain to make their festoons. We too use festoons, but ours are made of paper – your paper-chains, for instance.'

'We are doing what people did hundreds and hundreds of years ago then, when we hang up our paper-chains, for our festoons, and put up evergreens,' said Susan. 'Do you know anything else about the holly, Daddy?'

'Well, there are curious old tales or legends about it,' said Daddy. 'One is that the crown of thorns that Christ was made to wear was of holly, and that the blood the thorns caused, made the berries scarlet.'

Ann remembered how scarlet her blood had gleamed when she had pricked it with the holly. She was sad when she thought of such a cruel crown for Jesus.

'Another old tale tells about the robin and how he got his red breast,' said Daddy.

'How did he?' asked Peter, looking at a robin who had flown down nearby, hoping for a crumb or two.

'Well, a robin saw Jesus on the cross,' said Daddy, 'and he noticed his crown of thorns. The little bird saw how the thorns pricked Christ's brow, and he flew down to try and peck them out. He stained his breast in the blood of Jesus, and made it red – and, as you see, it is still red to this day.'

'That's a nice old legend,' said Susan. 'I can quite well imagine a robin doing a thing like that, Daddy – they are such friendly little creatures aren't they?'

'Yes, they are,' said her father. 'I suppose that is why we put them on Christmas cards. Also because they are still with us at Christmas-time. They seem to suit the kindly, friendly spirit of Christmas-time.'

'Here's a big crumb for you, robin red-breast,' called Ann, and threw out a bit of biscuit. The robin flew down to it, gave a little creamy carol, picked it up and flew off with it.

'I love his rich little voice,' said Susan. 'Well, Daddy – shall we go back to the holy tree, now, to "Christ's thorn", and cut a few more sprays for decoration?'

'We will,' said Daddy, and up they all got, leaving the summer-house to the little robin, who at once flew down and perched on the handle of the empty cocoa-jug.

Soon they had finished cutting the holly, and they took it into the house to put up.

'A big bunch over the doorway, please,' said Mother.

'That's where the old, old folk used to hang evergreens,' said Daddy, laughing. 'Here you are – here's a lovely bunch for the doorway.'

'I'll decorate the pictures in the hall,' said Susan. 'Ann, you go up to the nursery with these little sprays and do your share there.'

'And here's a beautiful piece for the pudding,' said Daddy, taking the little berried spray from his coat.

'How lovely the holly looks, shining brightly all round the rooms!' said Mother. 'Now – what about some mistletoe? You had better get that after dinner. There's not enough time now.'

'Right,' said everyone. And after dinner off they trooped to get the mistletoe.

The Curious Mistletoe

Forth to the wood did merry-men go
To gather in the mistletoe.

Walter Scott

'I do think it's funny to see the mistletoe growing so high up, on another tree,' said Ann, puzzled, when she and the others stood, after dinner, in the farmer's field, looking up at a great tuft of mistletoe growing on an oak tree.

'Well, it's what we call a *parasite*,' said Daddy, leaning the tall ladder against the sturdy oak tree.

'What's that?' asked Peter.

'A parasite is something that lives and feeds on something else,' said Daddy. 'It gets its food from its *host*, as we call the plant or animal it lives on.'

'Does the mistletoe find its food in the oak tree, then?' asked Susan. 'How does it?'

'The seed sends down little threads or *sinkers*,' said her father, climbing up the ladder. 'These sink into the branch of the tree, and feed on the sap there. Then up come two rather dingy green leaves, and hey presto! that is the beginning of one of the great tufts of mistletoe you see up here!'

'I'm coming up the ladder too,' said Benny. 'I'll throw down what you cut to the others.'

Daddy had to climb right into the tree to get to the mistletoe. It stuck out of the trunk and branches of the oak in great, bushy tufts. It glistened with pearly berries.

'It's not really very pretty,' said Benny, throwing down a big piece to the others. 'Not nearly so pretty as the holly. Why do we have it for decoration? I suppose there are all kinds of tales about the mistletoe too.'

'Oh yes,' said Daddy. 'I'll tell you them this evening, after tea. Now – here's a nice bit – catch!'

'We'll hang that up in the front porch,' cried Susan, as it came down to her. 'People always kiss each other under the mistletoe, Daddy, don't they? Do you know why?'

'Well, the mistletoe was dedicated to the goddess of love in the old days,' said Daddy, coming down the ladder, 'so I suppose it was natural to kiss under the mistletoe.'

'What a nice lot we've got,' said Ann, picking up the pearly sprays. 'Does it only grow on oak trees, Daddy?'

'It grows on poplars too,' said her father, 'and on apple trees, hawthorn and lime trees as well. It is only *half* a parasite really, because it has green leaves which do work like the green leaves of other plants. But its sinkers steal sap, as I told you before.'

'Who plants the mistletoe?' said Benny, puzzled. 'And how is it planted? Did the farmer plant it on these trees?'

'Oh no, Benny!' said Daddy, laughing. 'Of course not. The birds plant the mistletoe. The mistle-thrush plants most of it, I suppose.'

'However does it do that?' said Benny, astonished.

'Well, the mistle-thrush is very fond of the mistletoe berries,' said Daddy. 'He feasts on them, and then finds that some of the seeds have stuck to his beak. Squash a mistletoe berry, will you – and see how sticky it is.'

Each of the children squeezed a berry between finger and thumb. 'Gracious! It's as sticky as glue!' said Ann.

'Yes – the seeds are very very sticky,' said Daddy. 'Well,

when the thrush finds his beak sticky with them, he flies off to a tree and wipes his beak carefully on a bough to clean it. He probably leaves behind one or two of the sticky seeds. They don't fall off the bough – they stick there tightly.'

'And they grow there!' cried Peter. 'So that's how the mistle-thrush plants them – but he doesn't know it.'

'He certainly doesn't know it,' said Daddy, smiling. 'He flies off with a nice clean beak. The seeds he has left roll stickily down to the under part of the bough, stay there for a while, and then send out their sinker-threads. As soon as they reach the sap in the bough, they are able to feed on it and make leaves – then up grows a mistletoe bush, and when it has its berries, along comes the mistle-thrush and has a feast again!'

'I could plant some mistletoe myself, couldn't I?' said Ann, pressing a seed into a crack on the underside of an oak branch. 'There, sticky seed. Hold on tightly, put out your sinkers, and grow into a mistletoe bush for me, just for me.'

The others laughed. 'I suppose you think that by tomorrow there will be a nice big tuft of mistletoe for you, complete with berries!' said Peter. 'It will take ages to grow, won't it, Daddy?'

'Yes,' said his father, 'but no doubt in a few years there will be a nice little mistletoe plant there for Ann, and she will be very proud to pick it.'

'We've got enough mistletoe now, haven't we?' said Susan. 'Let's take it indoors. Daddy, did the early Christians use mistletoe? Is that why we put it up at Christmas-time?'

'Oh, mistletoe has been a holy and sacred plant for thousands of years,' said Daddy. 'Long before Jesus Christ was born. Christians took over a great many old customs and used them in their own way. Some of the things we do in our Christian religion were done by pagan peoples centuries before Jesus came – for old customs are difficult to kill.'

'Yes – I suppose it's better to keep old customs, and give them a new meaning,' said Susan, wisely.

'That's very well put,' said her father, pleased. 'That's exactly what you might say about the mistletoe. Centuries and centuries ago, the Druids, who were the priests of the folk of long ago, worshipped the oak tree, and worshipped also the mistletoe that grew on it.'

'Did they really?' said Peter. 'It seems odd to worship trees.'

'Oh, people have worshipped and prayed to many odd things,' said Daddy. 'The sun – and the moon – and the stars – trees and animals – all kinds of things, even idols of stone and wood that they themselves have made.'

'Still, it does seem queer to worship a funny plant like mistletoe, just because it grew on the sacred oak,' said Peter. 'I wouldn't have, if I'd lived in those days!'

'Oh yes you would!' said Daddy. 'You believe what you are taught, no matter in what century you live. There are very few people who are strong enough to think out everything for themselves, so nearly all of us believe what we are told to believe, worship what we see other people worshipping, and follow the customs we have known from childhood.'

'Well, anyway I shall find out if I can how all these old customs began,' said Peter, stoutly. 'I don't believe that mistletoe is sacred and ought to be worshipped, but I like to know who first taught that it should be.'

'Quite right,' said Daddy. 'Find out all you can. Well, as I said, the old priests, the Druids, worshipped the mistletoe

*The Druids worshipped the mistletoe because it grew on their
sacred tree, the oak*

because it grew on their sacred tree, the oak. They used to chant songs and carols when they cut sprays to hang up at their festivals – just as we cut it now to hang up at our festival at Christmas-time.'

'Why did the long-ago folk think that they ought to worship the mistletoe, just because it grew on the oak?' wondered Susan.

'Well, one reason was that the oak-leaves died in the winter, but the mistletoe on the oak remained green as you see it now,' said Daddy, beginning to walk home again. 'So they said "Ah, the life of the oak had gone into the mistletoe. The spirit of the oak is in that tuft. We must be careful of it, and worship it, for it now contains the life of the sacred oak." Then, when the leaves of the oak grew green again, they said that the life of the oak had gone from the mistletoe back to the tree.'

'What queer ideas,' said Susan. 'Of course *we* know that the mistletoe is only a half-parasite, planted by a bird – so we don't have those strange ideas.'

'The mistletoe had always been used as a kind of charm by peoples of many countries,' said her father. 'Sometimes it was used for driving away evil spirits. Sometimes the leaves were powdered and scattered over the fields to make crops grow well. Sometimes hunters carried a sprig of it hoping that it would give them success in their hunting!'

'I think *I* shall wear a sprig and see if it brings *me* good luck,' said Ann, at once. She broke off a little spray and stuck it into her hat. 'There. We'll see if the mistletoe is still as lucky as the old folk used to think!'

Everyone laughed. 'Ann *would* do something like that,' said Susan. 'Is the mistletoe supposed to do anything else queer, Daddy?'

'It was supposed to open all locks and doors,' said her father, opening the gate of their garden.

'Oh,' said Peter, 'perhaps it would open my old money-box, Daddy. I've lost the key.'

'Well really!' said Daddy. 'I'm not telling you all these things for you to try out yourselves. I'm only telling you what

Ann broke off a little spray and stuck it into her hat

long-ago, ignorant people believed in the childhood of the world.'

'I know,' said Peter. 'But I'll just *see* if the mistletoe will open that box.'

Mother came to meet them. 'What a long time you have been,' she said.

'Well – we had a lot to talk about,' said Susan. 'Mother, Daddy knows such a lot about the mistletoe.'

'Well, does he know why we are supposed to hang it from

something, instead of putting it behind pictures as we do holly?' said Mother, laughing. 'Can he tell me that? No one has ever told me why.'

'Yes, I can tell you,' said Daddy. 'It once killed a beautiful god, called Balder, and ever since then it has been made to grow high on a tree, out of harm's way. It must not touch the earth or anything on it – so we have to hang it, instead of letting it rest against our walls. Ah – I knew that, you see.'

'Who was Balder?' asked Susan, who was always on the look-out for a story.

'I'll tell you after tea,' said Daddy. 'My voice is getting hoarse from talking so much. Wait till we're sitting round the fire, and I'll tell you.'

Balder the Bright and Beautiful

'Twixt heaven and earth hangs mistletoe
Since Balder fell beneath its blow.

After tea the children pulled their father's chair near to the fire. Ann fetched his pipe. Peter put his tobacco pouch beside him.

'This is all very touching,' said Daddy, with a laugh. 'I suppose it means that you want the story of Balder.'

'Of course,' said Ann, getting on to his knee. 'You tell stories so nicely, Daddy. Fill your pipe and begin.'

Daddy began to fill his pipe, thinking hard.

'Who *was* Balder?' asked Peter.

'Well,' said Daddy, and he began the story of

BALDER THE BRIGHT AND THE BEAUTIFUL

Once upon a time, so the old Norsemen say, there lived many gods and goddesses, some good and some bad. They lived in the city of Asgard, and they were very powerful. There were great giants in those days too, strong and mighty, living in the ice country.

Odin was the chief of the gods, and lovely Frigga was his wife. They sat on their thrones in Valhalla, in the lovely city of Asgard.

The best-loved god of all was Balder the bright and the

beautiful. He was Frigga's son, and she loved him dearly. All the gods loved Balder, and the men and women of the earth loved him too, and even the stony giants.

His face was dazzling to look at, for he was very beautiful, and very kind. To see Balder was like seeing the bright sun, warm and lovely.

One night Balder had a strange and frightening dream. When he awoke his heart felt heavy. 'There is a shadow there,' said Balder, and he pressed his hand to his heart. 'I must go to my mother, Frigga. Maybe she will tell me what the shadow is. I have dreamed a dreadful dream, and it has left its shadow behind.'

Balder arose and went to find his mother, Frigga. She sat on her throne, looking out over the heavens. Balder lay down at her feet, sad and gloomy.

'Balder, what is the matter?' said Frigga, in the greatest surprise, for never before had the god looked so unhappy.

'Mother, I have a shadow in my heart,' said Balder, and took his mother's hand in his. He pressed it to his heart, and she felt the heavy shadow there. She grew very pale, and stood up in fear.

'My son, my son!' she said. 'It is the shadow of death!'

'If death comes to me, I will meet it bravely,' said Balder; but his bright face shone no more.

'You shall not die!' said Frigga. 'I am the queen, and everything must obey me. I will send word for everything on the earth to come to me, and I will make them promise not to hurt you, Balder, my son. Then, if you cannot be hurt, you cannot be killed.'

Frigga did not waste a moment. She sent out her commands at once. 'Tell everything on the earth to come before me,' she said. 'And, when they are before me, they must swear to me never to hurt Balder the bright and beautiful.'

Then all things on the earth came to her as she commanded. Every one of them swore an oath never to harm Balder.

Fire, water, iron and all metals, stones and earth, trees, sicknesses, poisons, beasts, birds and creeping things, all bowed down before Frigga, and promised her what she wanted. Then the queen of Asgard was happy again, and smiled at Balder her beloved son.

'You are safe, my son,' she told him. 'Now nothing can harm you.'

But Balder still felt the heavy shadow in his heart, and was sad. 'It will go,' said Frigga. 'There is nothing that can bring you death.'

The gods soon heard that everything on earth had promised not to hurt Balder. 'Does that mean that a spear will not wound him, that a stone will not bruise him?' they said to one another.

'Even so,' said Balder. 'You can try to spear me or cut me with your swords, but you cannot hurt me, for they are made of things that have promised my mother, Frigga, never to harm me.'

'Let us play a new game,' said the gods. 'Let us take Balder to the green that is outside the city of Asgard, and stand him there in the middle of it. Then let us take our weapons and hurl them at Balder. It will be strange to see them fall to the ground without harming him.'

So they took Balder to the green and put him in the middle. He stood there laughing, his face bright once more, for he had forgotten the shadow in his heart in the joy of the game.

The gods took their great spears, sharp-pointed and

strong. One after another they hurled them at Balder. But how strange – every spear glanced away and fell clanging to the ground. Not one would hurt Balder.

Then the gods took their swords, and they hacked at Balder, who stood laughing there. But not one sword would touch him, for the metal had promised never to harm him. They slipped aside from Balder, and no matter how hard the gods tried, they could not cut him with their swords.

Then they brought out their staves, great sticks of wood, heavy and strong. They struck at Balder with these, but the staves broke in half and would not hurt him.

'You cannot hurt me,' laughed Balder. 'You will only tire yourselves.'

But the sport was a good one, and the gods went on with the game for a long time, laughing and shouting.

n a great wolf

Then a wicked god called Loki heard the shouting and wondered what it was all about. He went near to see. He was amazed when he saw that the gods were trying to spear and cut Balder the bright and the beautiful.

'Now what is this?' said Loki to the laughing gods. 'Do you love Balder no more? You will kill him!'

'We cannot,' said the panting gods. 'Everything has promised Frigga that it will not harm Balder. See, we throw our spears, hack at him with our swords, and strike at him with our staves. But everything keeps its promise to Frigga, and will not hurt him.'

Loki was jealous of the beautiful god Balder. He was jealous of his beauty, and jealous of the love that everyone gave him. He wondered if it were really true that everything had promised not to hurt Balder.

'I will ask Frigga,' he said. But he did not dare to go to the queen of Asgard as himself, for Frigga did not like Loki. So he dressed himself as an old, old woman, and went to the palace where Frigga had her throne.

Loki came before the kindly Frigga, looking like a poor old woman. Frigga bade her sit down, and they began to talk.

'Have you come from far?' asked Frigga.

'Yes,' said Loki, 'and I saw a strange sight before I entered the gates of Asgard.'

'What was that?' asked Frigga.

'I saw Balder the bright and the beautiful, standing in the midst of the green,' said Loki, 'and behold, all the gods were hurling their spears and staves at him, but Balder stood there, laughing, unhurt.'

'That is a new sport for the gods,' said Frigga, smiling. 'Everything has promised me never to hurt my son Balder, so it matters not what they throw at him, he cannot be killed.'

'Did you say that *every*thing has promised you, every single thing?' said Loki.

'Only one thing did not promise,' said Frigga. 'And that is so small and weak that I did not ask it to. It cannot hurt Balder.'

'What is that one thing?' asked Loki, in a low voice, wondering if Frigga would tell him.

But Frigga had no idea that this was Loki, the wicked god, in front of her. She merely thought him to be a poor, simple old woman, and she answered him freely.

'That one thing is the little mistletoe plant. It grows in the palace gardens, and is so small that I did not bother to ask it to promise. How could it hurt my brave son Balder?'

This was all that Loki wanted to know. With shining eyes he left the queen of Asgard, and went into the palace gardens. He changed himself back into his own shape and looked about for the mistletoe plant.

He soon found it, growing small and sturdily in a strong tuft. He cut it, and made a short but very strong stave. Then he hurried to join the gods.

They were still playing their new game, for they had not yet tired of it. Loki went up to them and watched. He did not dare to hurl the mistletoe stick himself, for surely the gods would all fall upon him in anger if he hurt their beloved Balder. No – someone else must throw the stick.

He looked round the ring of laughing gods and there saw blind Hodur, the twin brother of Balder. Hodur loved Balder, and was sad that he could not see this new game, nor join in it. Loki went up to him quietly.

'Would you too like to throw something at Balder?' he said. 'You must not be left out. I will put a stick into your hand to throw.'

'I cannot see to throw. You know that well,' said Hodur.

'I can guide your aim,' said Loki. 'Draw back your arm, Hodur, and hurl the stick with all your might, for it will not hurt Balder. I will guide you.'

Hodur did as Loki said. He drew back his arm, and threw the stick of mistletoe with all his strength. Loki guided his arm, and the stick flew straight at Balder.

It struck him on the heart, and pierced it. Balder gave a terrible cry, and fell to the earth at once. The gods stared in amazement, puzzled and alarmed.

'What is it? Tell me,' cried blind Hodur, knowing by his

brother's cry that he had been grievously wounded. 'Balder, speak to me!'

But Balder could speak no more. He was dead. The gods lifted him up in horror, weeping for him, and Hodur, stretching out his hands in front to feel his way, tried to go to Balder too.

The gods went back to the city of Asgard. They came to Valhalla, and saw Frigga there, seated on her throne. How were they to tell her? But she saw their tearful eyes, and she knew that something terrible had happened.

'Balder the bright and beautiful is dead!' went the whisper round Asgard. 'Loki it was that killed him. Balder is dead!'

Hodur, filled with anger and grief, sought everywhere for Loki to punish him. But that clever god had slipped away, and no one knew where he hid.

'How could I have thrown that stave at my beloved brother?' said Hodur, and he wept bitterly. 'Why did I not guess that Loki meant to kill him?'

Balder's body was taken to the seashore. His ship, called Ringhorn, was there to take him on his last journey. It was the biggest ship in the world.

It was the Norse custom to place a dead man on his own ship, then set fire to it, and let the burning ship sail away on the sea. But Ringhorn, Balder's ship, would not move away from the shore.

'Send for the giantress, Hyrrockin,' said Odin. 'She must push the great ship out to sea for us.'

So a messenger was sent to the giantess, and soon she came riding up on a great wolf.

'Push my son Balder's ship out to sea,' said Odin. So Hyrrockin caught hold of the ship with her two great hands,

and pushed it so strongly that it sped down the rollers to the
sea, fire flashing beneath it as it went. The whole earth shook
as the ship took the sea.

Blazing high, it floated out on the waves, till it was lost to
sight in the coming night. So passed Balder the bright and
the beautiful.

Then Frigga took the mistletoe and planted it high on a
tree, so that never again could it touch the earth, and bring
harm to anyone. And, to this day, the mistletoe still grows
high in the branches of trees.

There was a pause at the end of the story. No one had
interrupted at all. Ann looked rather solemn.

'Oh Daddy – what a lovely story! But I didn't want the
mistletoe to kill Balder.'

'I know,' said Daddy, 'but I can't alter the story, I'm
afraid.'

All the children looked up at the bunch of mistletoe hanging down from the light, its pearly berries gleaming grey-
green.

'We know a lot about you now, Mistletoe!' said Peter.
'What an old, old plant you are, and what an old, old story
you have. Next time we kiss under the mistletoe we'll think of
your strange history.'

'And now it's time for bed, Ann,' said Mother.
'Tomorrow we'll have a lovely time, dressing the Christmas
tree!'

The Christmas Tree

And now the fir tree . . .
Acclaimed by eager, blue-eyed girls and boys,
Bursts into tinsel fruit and glittering toys,
And turns into a pyramid of light.

Eugene Hamilton

The children did not forget that the Christmas tree was to be dressed the next day. This was a job they all loved. The tree always looked so pretty when it was dressed in ornaments and candles, and had the fairy doll at the top under the silver star.

'I think it's the prettiest tree in the world when the candles are lighted from top to bottom, and shine and glow,' said Susan. 'I like them so much better than the artificial coloured lights some people have. The candles seem alive somehow.'

'Where are the ornaments?' said Peter. 'I'll get them.'

'Up in a box in the loft,' said Mother. 'Now be careful how you go up and down that steep ladder, Peter. We don't want you with a broken leg for Christmas.'

'I'll be all right!' said Peter, and sped up to the loft. He liked the loft. It was dim and dusty and smelt old. He picked his way between trunks and boxes, and then saw the big cardboard box in which the Christmas things were stored from year to year. He lifted up the lid.

'Yes – there are the glass ornaments – and there's the fairy doll, as pink and pretty as ever – and there's the silver star, still as bright – and oh, what a lovely lot of little coloured candles and candle-clips!' said Peter.

He took the box carefully down the ladder, then down the stairs and into the hall, where the others were bringing in the Christmas tree.

'Oh, what a lovely big one!' cried Peter, in excitement. 'It's bigger than last year's, I'm sure it is. Isn't it a beauty?'

It really was. It was in the wooden tub that was used year after year. The children would soon wrap red, crinkled paper round it to make it gay. They put the tree in its place, and it towered up high, taller than any of the children.

'Now we'll dress you,' cried Ann, dancing round. 'You are just an ordinary tree now, green and rather dull, with funny leaves that prick. But soon you will be a fairy tree, a magic tree, the prettiest tree in the world!'

'Hark at Ann,' said Benny. 'Come on, Ann, stop dancing about and get to work. Look, you can hang some of this silver tinfoil in thin strips all over the tree – that will make it look as if it is covered with little icicles. And after that you can put bits of cotton-wool on it here and there so that it looks as if snow has fallen on the branches.'

'Don't put the cotton-wool on till I've clipped on the candles in case it catches fire.'

'I'll hang the ornaments,' said Benny. 'I can reach nice and high. Oh – here's the red bell that looked so pretty last year – and the green ball – and here's the silver bird with a long tail, look. Hardly anything has been broken.'

'It's a well-shaped tree,' said Mother, coming up. 'It will look lovely when it's finished.'

'It's a fir-tree, isn't it?' asked Susan, busy clipping on the coloured candleclips, ready for the gay candles.

'Yes – the Christmas tree is always the same kind of tree,' said Mother. 'It's a spruce fir. You can tell a spruce because it has a spike at the top, sticking straight up to the sky.'

'Yes – very useful to tie a fairy doll to,' said Susan, looking at the straight spike at the top of their Christmas tree. 'Mother, who thought of the first Christmas tree? It's such a good idea.'

'It is, isn't it,' said Mother, cutting some coloured string into small pieces, so that she might tie small presents on the tree. 'Well, I don't exactly know who thought of the first Christmas tree, as *we* know it – but there is rather a nice old story about it.'

'Tell us, please!' said Ann, who loved a story of any kind. So Mother began the story.

One stormy Christmas Eve long, long ago, a forester and his family were sitting together round a big fire. Outside, the wind blew, and the snow made the forest white.

Suddenly there came a knock at the door. The family looked up, startled. 'Who can be in the forest at this time of the night?' said the forester, in surprise, and got up to open the door.

Outside stood a little child, shivering with cold, tired out and hungry. The forester picked him up in amazement, and brought him into the warm room.

'See,' he said, 'it is a little child. Who can he be?'

'He must remain here for the night,' said his wife, feeling the child's ice-cold hands. 'We will give him hot milk to drink, and a bed to sleep in.'

'He can have my bed,' said Hans, the forester's son. 'I can sleep on the floor tonight. Let us put the child into my warm bed.'

Outside stood a little child, shivering with cold

So the hungry, cold child was fed and warmed, and put into Hans' bed for the night. Then the family went to sleep, Hans on the floor beside the fire.

In the morning the forester awoke, and heard an astonishing sound. It seemed to him as if a whole choir of voices was singing. He awoke his wife, and she too heard the sweet singing.

'It is like the singing of angels,' whispered the forester. Then they looked at the child they had sheltered for the night, and saw that his face was dazzling bright. He was the Christ-child Himself!

In awe and wonder the forester and his family watched

the Holy Child. He went to a fir tree, and broke off a branch. He planted the branch firmly in the ground.

'See,' He said, 'you were kind to me, and you gave me gifts of warmth and food and shelter. Now here is my gift to you – a tree that at Christmas-time shall bear its fruit, so that you may always have abundance.'

And so, at Christmas-time, the Christmas tree shines out in beauty, and bears gifts of many kinds.

Mother stopped and looked round. The children were all listening, and for the moment had forgotten their task of decorating the tree.

'That was a nice story,' said Ann. 'I wish the Christ-child had come to *me*. I would have given up my bed to Him, and He could have had my toys as well.'

'Does the Christmas tree have real fruits?' asked Peter, trying to remember. 'This one hasn't any – only just its many branches of prickly leaves.'

'Oh, you must have seen the cones on the spruce firs,' said Susan. 'Surely you have! You know what fir-cones are, silly!'

'Of course!' said Peter, remembering. 'Yes – they hang down from the branches, don't they?'

'The cones of the spruce fir do, but not the cones of the silver fir,' said Benny, who was rather good at trees. 'They sit upright. You can always tell the spruce from the silver fir by its top, too – the spruce has a sharp spear-like point but the silver fir has a bushy top.'

'Oh, that's easy to remember,' said Ann. 'Why hasn't our Christmas tree any cones on it, Benny? I wish it had. I would paint them silver and make them look lovely!'

'Well, it's only a baby tree,' said Benny. 'It hasn't borne cones yet. If we plant it in the garden and let it grow year by year, it will grow cones, of course. Let's do that. It has good roots, and should be all right if we plant it out.'

'Then we can have the same tree year after year!' said Ann. 'I should like that.'

'I like its prickly needle-like leaves,' said Peter. 'See, Ann – they look as if someone had combed them neatly down the middle of the branch, and made a parting – just like you do to your hair!'

The others laughed. Peter was right – the little boughs did look as if someone had made a parting down the middle of the close-set needle-leaves.

'The fir tree isn't only useful as a Christmas tree,' said Mother. 'Its straight trunk is used for lots of things that need to be quite straight. Perhaps you can think of some.'

'Masts of ships!' said Benny at once.

'Telegraph posts!' said Susan.

'Scaffolding poles!' said Peter.

'You've all said what I was going to say,' said Ann. 'Are they right, Mother?'

'Quite right. The fir tree gives its trunk for all those things,' said Mother. 'People say that its name "fir" should really be "fire". It should be called the fire tree, not the fir tree, because once upon a time its gummy, resinous branches used to be broken off, lighted, and used as flaring torches.'

'Have you noticed that the fir tree's roots are very shallow?' said Benny, fixing a shining yellow ornament to a bough. 'They stand out above the ground in the wood. I should think the firs would easily fall in a strong storm.'

'Oh, they do,' said Mother. 'And sometimes, if one fir falls, it knocks down the next, and that one falls and knocks down a third tree, and so they may go on, all through the forest, making quite a path of fallen trees.'

'Like a row of dominoes each knocking down the next,' said Ann, remembering how she often stood up her dominoes in a row, and then touched the first one, which caused the whole row to fall, one after the other.

'I'm going to put the star on the top of the tree now,' said Benny, fetching a chair. 'Mother, I suppose we put a star at the top to represent the Star of Bethlehem, don't we?'

'Yes,' said Mother. 'The Christmas tree should always have the Star of Bethlehem shining at the top.'

'Have we had the custom of decorating the Christmas tree for hundreds and hundreds of years, just as we have had for the holly and mistletoe?' said Ann.

'Oh dear me no!' said Mother. 'It's not much more than a hundred or so years ago that the first Christmas tree was set up in England. It was first known in Germany, then spread to other countries, and at length came to England. It is the kind of simple and beautiful idea that spreads into all lands. Who first thought of it we don't really know, nor quite how long ago. The idea itself may be old, but our English custom is certainly not older than the last century. Prince Albert the husband of Queen Victoria, set up a Christmas tree at Windsor in 1841 – and after that the tree was used in England.'

'It must be nice to begin a custom like this,' said Ann. 'I wish I could begin one of my own. Mother, can I put the candles into Susan's clips?'

'Isn't the tree beginning to look lovely?' said Susan, stepping back a little to see it. 'How the ornaments shine – and

*Prince Albert, the husband of Queen Victoria, set up a Christmas
Tree at Windsor*

the tinfoil strips gleam – and the star glitters. I'm longing for the time when the candles will all be lighted.'

It took the children all the morning to decorate the tree properly, but they loved every minute of it. By the time it was finished there was not a bough without a candle, present or ornament, and the frosted cotton-wool and strips of tinfoil gave the tree a glitter and shine that made it very beautiful.

The star shone at the top, and under it stood the fairy doll, a silver crown on her head, silver wings behind her and a silver wand in her hand. Little presents for every member of the household hung here and there, wrapped in coloured paper.

'They are *proper* presents,' said Mother, 'not useful gifts, which should never be put on a Christmas tree, according to old beliefs – but beautiful little gifts which will bring joy and pleasure to everyone.'

'How lovely!' said Ann, dancing round. 'Now the tree is beautiful. Mother, I wouldn't be surprised if all the other trees in the garden came close to the window and looked in when we light our Christmas tree!'

'You do say funny things,' said Benny, laughing, but they all thought secretly that it was rather a quaint idea of Ann's, and could quite imagine the hollies and the yews, the birches and the oaks pressing themselves against the window to see the beauty of the lighted Christmas tree.

'It's finished, it's finished!' said Ann. 'Now it only has to wait in patience to be lighted from top to toe.'

'I'm so hungry,' said Peter. 'I say – what are we going to do after lunch?'

'I'm going to do some more Christmas cards,' said Susan, 'and wrap up some presents. And I am making some crackers too – though I haven't any "cracks" to put into them to go pop when they are pulled. But I know how to make lovely crackers. We did some at school this term.'

'Well – you will be very busy,' said Mother. 'I will come and help you all. We will have a nice Christmassy afternoon!'

A Christmassy Afternoon

Then the grim boar's head frowned on high,
Crested with bays and rosemary.

There the huge sirloin reeked hard by,
Plum porridge stood, and Christmas pie.

Walter Scott

It was snowing when the children settled down that afternoon to finish off their Christmas preparations. The next day
was Christmas Eve – a most exciting day, when presents
were labelled and hidden away for Christmas morning, and
when stockings were hung up at night.

'What lovely cards you do,' said Ann, looking over Susan's
shoulder at the card she was painting very neatly. 'I do like
that robin – and the snow on the roofs of the houses is very
real.'

'It's the printing that spoils my cards,' said Susan. 'I can't
seem to print nearly as neatly as Benny.'

Benny's cards were certainly beautifully done. His Christmas messages inside were printed in gold ink, the capitals
outlined in black or red.

Ann and Peter had finished their cards and posted them.
They felt quite glad that the elder children hadn't seen them,
because they were not nearly so beautiful as theirs.

The mantelpiece was full of cards that had come for the
children. Downstairs Mother's mantelpiece and bookcases

were covered with them too. They were so gay, all sizes and shapes and colours. Some were very plain and neat, others were merry and bright.

The children loved the cards. They looked at each one carefully, and always read the little messages inside. They thought cards at Christmas were a very good idea.

Mother was sitting by the fire, doing some mending. The children liked having her there. They could ask her how to spell words, and could show her their cards as they finished them.

'Who first thought of Christmas cards?' said Susan, drawing a very fat and cheerful-looking robin. 'Is it a very old custom, Mother, like the others we've heard about?'

'No, it isn't,' said Mother. 'I do know a little about Christmas cards, because your great-grandfather's was one of the first firms to print them. But the first cards were not printed, they were written.'

'How do you mean?' asked Benny.

'Well, at the beginning of the last century, schoolboys had to write compositions and decorate the sheets of paper on which they wrote them, in order to show their parents how they had improved in their writing,' said Mother. 'They took these Christmas compositions home with them, and presented them to their parents, who, of course, were proud of them, and stood them up on the mantelpiece for everyone to see.'

'Oh – like you stand up my drawings that I bring home from school!' said Ann.

'Yes,' said Mother. 'Well, for some years these Christmas papers were done by schoolboys, and then a few grown-ups thought it would be a good idea if they too sent Christmas messages, handwritten on decorated paper, to their friends.

A schoolboy brings home his Christmas composition

So they did, and these private Christmas greetings became quite popular.'

'And so, I suppose, people then began to have them printed?' said Benny, looking up.

'Yes,' said his mother. 'It became the fashion to send a printed card with a Christmas greeting on it to friends – it was a simple and kindly way of remembering them at Christmas-time. At first, of course, the cards were very very simple – just a sprig of holly or mistletoe, or a little fat robin like the one on Susan's cards.'

'Then did they get like the ones we have now, Mother?'

said Ann, looking at the brilliant array on the mantelpiece. 'Really, some of the cards sent aren't a bit Christmassy, just pretty pictures that could be sent at any time of the year.'

'Well, there were all kinds of fashions in cards,' said Mother. 'Wait, I've got a few old ones that Grandfather gave me. Fetch me the box on the top shelf of the bookcase in my room, Benny.'

Benny fetched it and Mother opened it. In it were some old Christmas cards. Some of the oldest were, as Mother had said, quite simple and plain – but then came glittering ones, frosted all over. Ann liked those.

'These are nice,' she said. 'See how they shine. The frost must be stuck on. It rubs off a bit when I scratch it with my nail. Look, my finger is shining with it. I like these frosted cards, Mother.'

'Your great-grandfather used to send these to his friends,' said Mother. 'And now look at these silk-fringed ones. We don't see these nowadays. Grandfather had them sent to him. I suppose you like these too, Ann?'

Ann did, though Susan thought they were too elaborate. She liked something simpler.

'Then we had cards of coloured celluloid,' said Mother. 'You can still see them sometimes. But nowadays if we want a really nice card we choose a beautiful reproduction of the Nativity, or some fine religious picture – or we look for some really artistic card. We do not go in for show.'

'I like the cards *I* get,' said Ann, looking at hers that stood beside the clock. 'There's one that has a bear popping out with a Christmas message when you open it, Mother. And here's one I like – see, when it's opened, a Christmas tree stands up, with presents on! And here's one with a little window – when you open it, you see Santa Claus peeping out!'

'Yes – children's cards are amusing and clever nowadays,' said Mother, shutting up her box of old Christmas cards, with their glittering frost and silky fringes. 'Each generation has its own ideas, its likes and dislikes.'

'It's interesting to know that even a little thing like a Christmas card has its own history,' said Benny, finishing off a card with a flourish. 'Who did the very first card, I wonder?'

'I'm going to make my crackers now,' said Susan, getting out some red, yellow and green crinkled paper. 'Like to help me, Ann? Look, it's quite easy. I use this white paper for the lining – and put my little present inside – then I cut the crinkled paper to the right size – and roll it . . .'

'And nip it at the two ends – and tie the nips with that coloured tinsel thread,' said Ann. 'And then paste a scrap on the front. I didn't think it would be as easy as that to make crackers.'

'Mother, do you know the story of the Christmas cracker?' said Benny, beginning another card.

'No, I don't,' said Mother. 'I only know they are about a hundred years old. When I was a child they used to be called "bon-bons", and they had sweets inside.'

'I suppose they are called "crackers" because they go off with a crack when we pull them,' said Susan, sticking a scrap on to the first cracker she had made.

'Where are you going, Mother?' asked Ann, seeing her mother get up.

'Just to take the Christmas pudding off the stove,' said Mother. 'It will be nice and black for Christmas Day now.'

Mother came back after a while, and the children had more questions ready for her.

'Did we always have a feast at Christmas-time, for hundreds and hundreds of years?'

'Why do we have a turkey?'

'Why aren't there any plums in the plum pudding?'

'Is there any old reason for hiding things in the pudding?'

'How did mincepies begin?'

'My goodness me, I'm not an encyclopedia!' said Mother. 'Ah – listen – that's Daddy home early, I'm sure. You can pick *his* brains a little now, and give me a rest.'

So, when Daddy came in he was greeted by another list of Christmas questions. 'Why, why, why? When? How?'

'One question at a time!' he said. 'Yes, Christmas feasting is very old – but I daresay you children would have enjoyed it most in Queen Elizabeth's time. They really did know how to feast in those days. Even you, Peter, would have had more than enough to eat!'

Everyone laughed. Peter's enormous appetite was always a joke.

'Did they have the boar's head carried in, in those days?' asked Benny.

'The boar's head? Whatever's that?' said Ann, in surprise. 'What's a boar?'

'A pig,' said Daddy. 'Yes, at Christmas-time in the old days, servants carried in a great silver dish, wreathed with bay, on which was a roasted boar's head. In the boar's mouth was put an apple or a lemon, and its ears were decorated with sprigs of rosemary. Carols were sung as it was brought in – it was a great sight!'

'I wish I could see it,' said Peter, his eyes shining.

They really did know how to fea

'Well, if you were at Queen's College, Oxford, you could, because the old custom is still followed there,' said his father.

'Do they sing a carol when the boar's head is brought in?' asked Peter.

'Yes – it is in Latin – and the words mean something like this,' said Daddy.

> 'The Boar's head in hand bear I
> Bedecked with bays and rosemary;
> And I pray you, my masters, be merry,
> I bear the Boar's head,
> Rendering praise to the Lord.'

'Did they bring in turkeys too, in the old days with the

Queen Elizabeth's time

boar's head?' asked Ann. 'We've got a most enormous turkey hanging in the larder. I've seen it.'

'No, they didn't bring in turkeys,' said Daddy, 'that's quite a new custom, which we get from America. The goose used to be the bird we most often had at Christmas-time in England. But beef, the "Roast Beef of Olde England" has always been our greatest Christmas dish. We have always enjoyed our sirloin of beef – or our baron of beef which is two sirloins joined together.'

'Why is it called sirloin?' wondered Peter. 'We don't say sirloin of mutton, do we?'

'Well, you see, Charles II thought so much of loin of beef as a dish that he actually knighted it,' said Daddy, with a laugh. 'You can see him doing it, can't you – striking it with his sword, and saying "Rise, Sir Loin!"'

'Oh, is that really how the sirloin got its name?' said Peter, amused. 'Fancy knighting food you like. I've a good mind to knight chocolate ice-cream.'

'The king always has a baron of beef served on his table at Christmas-time,' said Mother. 'Dick, do you know anything about Christmas pudding? The children keep asking why it's called plum pudding when it has no plums in it. I suppose the old name contains its history.'

'Yes, it does,' said Daddy. 'In the old days the people at Christmas-time ate a dish called frumenty, which was really stewed wheat grains. This gradually became plum porridge, and then plum pudding. It was then made of beef or mutton broth thickened with brown bread, raisins, currants, prunes, spices and gingerbread.'

'Prunes are really plums, aren't they?' said Susan. 'Is that why the pudding was called plum pudding?'

'Well, people in those days used to call even raisins and currants "plums",' said Daddy. 'Now, of course, we don't even put prunes, or plums, into the pudding, so we really oughtn't to call it plum pudding at all. Christmas pudding is a much better name.'

'We don't put broth into the pudding either!' said Mother, 'and we do put into it a great many things that the old people never thought of – ground-up nuts, for instance – and . . .'

'And silver thimbles and threepenny bits and little horse-shoes for luck,' said Ann.

'Well, I don't know how *that* habit began,' said Daddy. 'I've never heard. It was probably started just for a joke, and was such fun that it became popular!'

'What about mince-pies?' said Peter. 'We're going to have some, aren't we Mother?'

'Of course!' said his mother. 'We couldn't have Christmas without mince-pies!'

'Well, you wouldn't have known the mince-pies of olden days,' said Daddy. 'They were pies *really* filled with minced meat, as their name tells you. The first minced-pies were filled with things like chopped-up hare, pheasant, capon, partridge and so on; then, later on, sweeter things were put into the pies, such as raisins, oranges, sugar and spices – but they were still called mince-pies, though there was no longer any minced meat in them.'

'Nowadays mince-pies are very sweet to the taste,' said Mother. 'They are a sweet-course, not a meat-course. You must all remember to eat your pies in silence, so that you may have happiness for a month next year, each time you eat a mince-pie!'

'Another old custom,' said Susan. 'I like that one. I don't know what Peter did last year, about his "happy-months", Mother, because he ate fourteen mince-pies, and there are only twelve months in a year.'

'Oh, the thirteenth and fourteenth pies ran into next year!' said Peter, grinning. 'I could do with a mince-pie this very minute!'

'Well, how funny – here is one for you!' said Mother. Sure enough, on a dish were piled the first mince-pies, one for everybody. How Peter's eyes gleamed.

'Good!' he said. 'Thank you, Mother. Just what I wanted. Now I'll be able to wish a happy month next year. That will take me to March!'

Susan put away her crackers. Benny put away his cards. They were all ready for tea. It was nice sitting there, the big fire glowing, and the holly round the walls, its berries shining red.

'Tomorrow is Christmas Eve!' said Susan. 'And we will bring in the old Yule log!'

Bringing in the Yule Log

Come bring with a noise,
My merry, merry boys,
The Christmas log to the firing.

Robert Herrick

The snow was falling again when the children looked out of the window after breakfast. It had fallen in the night, too, and the ground was white.

'The snow is thick enough for us to use sleighs,' said Benny, pleased: 'That will be an easy way to bring in the big Yule log, Mother. Has John cut it down for us?'

'Yes,' said Mother. 'It is at the top of the garden. You can go and see it, but you had better wait till Daddy comes home to bring it in. Then he can help to lift it on the big fire in the lounge. It is too heavy for you.'

'I don't know any family but ours that brings in the Yule log,' said Susan, as they went up the garden to see the great log waiting for them.

'Well, think of our big old fireplace in the lounge!' said Benny. 'You can only bring in a proper Yule log if you have a big enough fireplace to put it in. Daddy said last year that in the old days whole small trees were sometimes brought in and laid on the hearth, because in those days they had such enormous fireplaces.'

'Oh, yes, of course,' said Susan. 'I forgot that most people have small fireplaces. I'm glad we've got one big enough to bring in a proper Yule log and burn it on Christmas Eve.'

'Look – there it is,' said Ann, dancing up to it. 'What a beauty! It will just go into our hearth nicely – but Mother will have to have a very big fire ready to burn it!'

It really was a fine big log. John the gardener was nearby, and he smiled when he saw the children.

'There's a wonderful log for you,' he said. 'And I've got one for myself too, over yonder, look.'

He pointed to another log, not so long as theirs, but very big and broad.

'Oh, have you got a big enough fireplace in your old cottage?' asked Ann.

'Yes, I have,' said John. 'They built big chimneys in the days when my cottage was put up, and my kitchen hearth is half the kitchen. My, it's a warm place when we've got a log like that burning.'

'We could put our log on our sledge and drag it over the snow when Daddy comes,' said Peter. 'How are you going to get yours home, John?'

'I'll haul it behind me on a rope,' said John. 'It'll run easy enough on the snow. My old grandad, he used to haul in a Yule log each year too, and he used to light it with a bit of the old Yule log that he'd had the year before. Somehow he managed to keep a bit of it by him, and he always said that he lighted one Yule log from another, down the years.'

'Oh, I hadn't heard of that,' said Susan, pleased. 'We'll do that too. We'll keep a bit of this log till *next* Christmas, and then light the new one from it – and then we'll keep a bit of the next one, and light the following Yule log from that – and . . .'

'You needn't go on down the century,' said Benny, laughing. 'We know what you mean. We'll tell Mother, and get her to save a bit.'

'Why is it called the Yule log, John?' asked Ann, walking along the log. 'I know Yule means Christmas, but why do we call it the Yule log instead of the Christmas log?'

'You ask your father that,' said John. 'I've got no learning like that. All I know is that in days gone by bringing in the Yule log was a proper ceremony – you know, singing and merry-making and all. Seems like we've got no time for things like that nowadays.'

'We do other things instead,' said Benny. 'Did your grandfather follow other old customs as well as bringing in the Yule log, John?'

'Oh yes,' said John, beginning to saw some wood up. 'He went mumming.'

'Mumming? What's mumming?' said Peter, who had never heard the word.

'Oh, mummers got themselves all dressed up and went out singing and dancing round people's houses,' said John. 'Sometimes boys dressed up as girls, and girls as boys. I remember my grandfather saying he had to act about funny-like, and do a lot of made-up fighting.'

'I should like to go out mumming,' said Benny, thinking about it. 'And I'd like to wassail too!'

'Wassail? What a funny word! How do you wassail?' said Ann, jumping off the log.

'Wassailing is just drinking people's health out of the wassail bowl,' said Benny, rather grandly. 'It's a very old custom too, like mumming. People used to go wassailing at Christmas-time and New Year's Day. We don't do it now.'

'Let's go and make a snowman,' said Peter, not very interested in wassailing. 'Then we can have a snowfight.'

So they went off to play in the snow, leaving the Yule log to get white in the falling flakes. They forgot about it till their father came home to tea and wanted to know what they had done about the Yule log.

'Oh – it's up the garden,' said Benny. 'It's a beauty. It was too heavy to bring in alone. Let's go and get it now.'

'I've got a fine fire burning in the lounge hearth,' said Mother, stirring it up. 'Go and get the log now, before it is too dark, and we will put it on.'

'Then there will be a lovely fire for you to tell us the Christmas story by, and for us to sing carols round,' said Ann, rushing to get her coat.

Mother called out to them as they went out of the garden-door. 'I'll come and help. It's supposed to be bad luck if everyone doesn't help to bring in the Yule log.'

'Yes, come along,' cried the children.

So, with coats thrown round them, and scarves over their heads, everyone hurried up the snowy garden to where the Yule log lay, hidden under a thick covering of snow. Benny pulled his sledge behind him.

Somehow he and Daddy got the big, heavy log on to the sledge. Then, with everyone giving a hand to the ropes, the Yule log was brought triumphantly into the house. It was taken to the lounge, and rolled into the fire.

Sizzle, sizzle, sizzle, went the melting snow as the flames licked it away. Then, after a while, the log began to blaze, and soon was well alight. Everyone watched it with pleasure, especially the four children.

'Do you remember the story I told you of Balder the bright and the beautiful?' said their father, as they watched the log burn. 'Well, the old Norsemen, who believed in the

Everyone hurried up the snowy garden to where the Yule log lay

gods I told you about then, used to burn a log each year to the great god Thor, who also dwelt in Asgard.'

'Why is it called *Yule* log?' asked Benny.

'It probably comes from the name that the old Norsemen used to give Odin, the father of the gods,' said Daddy. 'He was called "Jul-Vatter" or "Yule-Father"; Yule was a word meaning "sun" and the god Odin was supposed to be the sun himself. The old Norsemen kept a festival of the sun just about this time of year – a "Jul" or Yule festival – so I suppose the name has come down through the years, and now means Christmas-time, which we hold at the same time as the old Norsemen held their sun or Yule festival.'

The log blazed up and sparks flew off. Mother turned out the light. 'We'll sit and watch it,' she said. 'It's a pretty sight, to see a big log burning.'

They all sat down, and watched the glowing fire. Susan told her father how John had said his grandfather had gone mumming.

'That's interesting,' said her father. 'Mumming is a very old custom, still in use in some parts of the country, but rapidly dying out now.'

'Is pantomime anything to do with mumming?' said Benny, getting a little farther back from the hot fire. 'They're both acting, aren't they?'

'Yes – but they are not the same thing,' said Daddy. 'Pantomime is acting in dumb show – no word should be spoken at all – that is true pantomime, and that is how pantomime began.'

'Good gracious!' said Susan, thinking of the lovely pantomimes she had seen, 'no word spoken! Why, in the pantomimes I have seen, the actors speak and sing all the time!'

'Yes, that is true,' said Daddy. 'So they shouldn't really be called pantomimes at all. If you had seen real pantomime in the long-ago days, you would simply have seen actors, not singers, or talkers – men coming on, acting in dumb show some well-known story, which could easily be followed by the delighted audience.'

'And that was the beginning of our gorgeous pantomimes!' said Susan, surprised. 'It doesn't seem possible.'

'Well, the early pantomime underwent all kinds of changes,' said her father. 'And different countries had different kinds. Gradually the dumb show altered – singing was brought in – masks were used – and at one stage pantomime became the ballet, which is again quite a different thing.'

'I like the pantomime as it is *now*,' said Ann, decidedly. 'I like all the singing and dancing and jokes, and those lovely scenes. Oh – do you remember, Susan, in *Cinderella* when the pumpkin and rats turned into a coach and horses? I did love that.'

'Yes, pantomime in our country is a very entertaining thing,' said Daddy. 'No other country has anything quite like it, with its gorgeous scenes, and its bits of fairy-tale interwoven here and there.'

'We're going after Christmas, aren't we?' said Ann, feeling excited at the very thought. 'We're going to see Aladdin and the Wonderful Lamp. I shall love that.'

The clock struck six. 'Well,' said Mother, 'what about a few carols? Then I will tell you the Christmas story as usual – and then – supper and bed-time!'

Christmas Carols

Then came the merry maskers in
And carols roared with blythesome din.

Walter Scott

'We ought really to dance while we sing the Christmas carols,' said Daddy, 'because the word "carol" means a ring-dance, a dance in a circle.'

'Did people dance in the churches in olden days then?' said Susan, astonished. 'Did they sing and dance at the same time?'

'Oh yes,' said Daddy. 'That was an old, old religious custom, which began long before Christ was born. Then, when the early Christians took over some of the old customs, and made them into Christian rites, singing and dancing was allowed in their churches too.'

'But we don't dance in church now,' said Benny.

'No, because it was forbidden years and years ago,' said his father. 'The word "carol" soon came to mean a merry song suggestive of dancing, a happy song, bringing in such things as the Nativity, or the shepherds or angels. We like to sing them at Christmas-time because it is a happy time, and we want merry, dancing tunes then.'

'I suppose our carols are very old,' said Susan.

'A good many of them are,' said Daddy. 'The man who really began the true carol was St Francis of Assisi, who was born in the twelfth century.'

'I know about St Francis,' said Ann. 'I've got a picture of him in my bedroom. He called Jesus our "Little Brother". Did St Francis make up some of our carols?'

'We don't know for certain,' said her father, 'but probably some of his companions did. Then, from Italy, where St Francis lived, the carol spread abroad, keeping its simplicity, religious feeling and merry spirit. There is another kind of carol we know too – the ones we call the "Nowells".'

'Oh yes – there's "The First Nowell",' said Ann. 'We'll sing it tonight – won't we, Mother?'

'We know a very popular carol that came from Bohemia,' said Daddy, 'all about a good king of Bohemia. Who knows the carol I mean?'

' "Good King Wenceslas",' said all the children at once.

'Right,' said their father. 'He was a real king, and his feast is held on St Stephen's Day, which is Boxing Day.'

'Boxing Day!' said Benny. 'Now what does *that* mean, Daddy? It has always seemed to be such a funny name for the day after Christmas. Do people go and watch boxing matches somewhere?'

They all laughed. 'Of course not, silly,' said Susan. 'It's because the postman and the dustman come round for their Christmas boxes, isn't it, Daddy?'

'Yes, it is,' said Daddy.

'But we don't give them boxes, we give them money,' said Ann, puzzled. 'Used they to get boxes instead?'

'No,' said Daddy. 'What happened was this – boxes were put into the churches for people to put money into to give to the poor. These boxes were opened on Christmas Day, and the next day the money was given to anyone in need.'

'Oh – so the day after Christmas was Box Money Day,' said Benny.

'Yes,' said Daddy, 'and in later years young apprentices took boxes round to their masters' customers, begging for money gifts, however small. The customers put money into these boxes – which, in those days were made of earthenware or porcelain, and could only be opened by being broken – and then the youngsters divided the money among themselves.'

'Well, it's easy to see how Boxing Day came to have its name then,' said Benny, 'with boxes for the poor in the churches, and boxes being taken round by apprentices. Our postman doesn't bring a box, though. He brings a bag for the money, and a book to put down the names of givers and the amount they give.'

'Yes – and even when the whole custom has completely died out, we shall still call the day after Christmas "Boxing Day",' said Mother. 'Always there are fingers of the past reaching out to us who live in the present.'

There came the sound of footsteps outside, and voices talking low. Then suddenly a carol was begun, and the family heard the sound of 'Good King Wenceslas' being vigorously sung. The carol-singers had arrived.

Good King Wenceslas look'd out
On the feast of Stephen;
When the snow lay round about,
Deep and crisp, and even:
Brightly shone the moon that night,
Though the frost was cruel,
When a poor man came in sight,
Gath'ring winter fuel.

*There came the sound of footsteps outside, and voices talking low;
the carol singers had arrived*

Solo 1.   'Hither, page, and stand by me,
        If thou know'st it, telling,
        Yonder peasant who is he!
        Where and what his dwelling!'

Solo 2.   'Sire, he lives a good league hence,
        Underneath the mountain;
        Right against the forest fence,
        By Saint Agnes' fountain.'

Solo 1.   'Bring me flesh, and bring me wine,
        Bring me pine-logs hither:
        Thou and I will see him dine,
        When we bear them thither.'

Chorus.   Page and monarch forth they went,
        Forth they went together:
    Through the rude wind's wild lament
        And the bitter weather.

Solo 2.   'Sire, the night is darker now,
        And the wind blows stronger,
    Fails my heart, I know not how:
        I can go no longer.'

Solo 1.   'Mark my footsteps, good my page;
        Tread thou in them boldly:
    Thou shalt find the winter's rage
        Freeze thy blood less coldly.'

Chorus.   In his master's steps he trod,
        Where the snow lay dinted;
    Heat was in the very sod
        Which the Saint had printed.
    Therefore, Christian men, be sure,
        Wealth or rank possessing,
    Ye who now will bless the poor,
        Shall yourselves find blessing.

The children joined in too, and then waited for the next carol. What was it to be?

'The first nowell the angels did say' began the clear young voices. Ann smiled. 'They've chosen a Nowell,' she whispered. 'Let's sing it too.'

So they did. After that there came a knock at the door. Mother opened it. 'We're collecting for the poor old people in this parish, to give them food and coals this winter,' said a voice. 'Please can you spare something?'

Mother gave them some silver. The carol-singers were pleased. They thanked her and went off to the next house.

'That is another very, very old custom,' said Daddy, 'singing carols for alms – getting money for charity. Even as far back as Norman times carol singers went out at Christmastime, and asked for money.'

'Well, now let *us* sing some, sitting round the blazing Yule log,' said Susan, her face glowing in the heat. 'I think this is nice, this custom of ours – sitting round a blazing log fire on Christmas Eve, all of us together, singing carols, and then listening to the old, old story.'

'We'll each choose a carol, as we always do,' said Mother. 'I'll chose "Hark, the Herald Angels Sing". I hope you all know the words.'

Then, ringing through the house went the six voices, Ann's a little out of tune, but just as loud as anyone else's.

> Hark! the herald Angels sing,
> Glory to the new-born King;
> Peace on earth, and mercy mild,
> God and sinner reconcil'd.
> > Hark! the herald angels sing,
> > Glory to the new-born King.

> Joyful all ye nations rise,
> Join the triumph of the skies,
> With the angelic host proclaim,
> Christ is born in Bethlehem.
> > Hark! the herald angels sing,
> > Glory to the new-born King.

> Christ by highest Heaven ador'd
> Christ the everlasting Lord!

Late in time behold Him come,
Offspring of a virgin's womb.
   Hark! the herald angels sing,
   Glory to the new-born King.

Hail the heaven-born Prince of Peace!
Hail the Sun of Righteousness!
Light and Life to all He brings,
Risen with healing on His wings.
   Hark! the herald angels sing,
   Glory to the new-born King.

Mild he lays his glory by,
Born that man no more may die,
Born to raise the sons of earth,
Born to give them second birth.
   Hark! the herald angels sing,
   Glory to the new-born King.

'That was lovely,' said Susan, when the carol was finished. 'I do like carols. They are so merry and the tune makes you want to dance. Now what shall we have?'

'Let's have "I saw three ships come sailing in, On Christmas Day, on Christmas Day",' said Ann. So they sang it lustily.

I saw three ships come sailing in
 On Christmas Day, on Christmas Day;
I saw three ships come sailing in
 On Christmas Day in the morning.

And what was in those ships all three,
 On Christmas Day, on Christmas Day?

And what was in those ships all three,
  On Christmas Day in the morning?

Our Saviour Christ and his lady,
  On Christmas Day, on Christmas Day;
Our Saviour Christ and his lady,
  On Christmas Day in the morning.

Pray whither sailed those ships all three,
  On Christmas Day, on Christmas Day;
Pray whither sailed those ships all three,
  On Christmas Day in the morning.

O, they sailed into Bethlehem,
  On Christmas Day, on Christmas Day;
O, they sailed into Bethlehem,
  On Christmas Day in the morning.

And all the bells on earth shall ring,
  On Christmas Day, on Christmas Day;
And all the bells on earth shall ring,
  On Christmas Day in the morning.

And all the angels in Heaven shall sing,
  On Christmas Day, on Christmas Day;
And all the angels in Heaven shall sing,
  On Christmas Day in the morning.

And all the souls on earth shall sing,
  On Christmas Day, on Christmas Day;
And all the souls on earth shall sing,
  On Christmas Day in the morning.

Then let us all rejoice amain,
    On Christmas Day, on Christmas Day;
Then let us all rejoice amain,
    On Christmas Day in the morning.

Then Peter had his turn, and he chose 'The first nowell the angel did say'.

The first nowell the angel did say
Was to three poor shepherds in the fields as they lay;
In fields where they lay keeping their sheep,
On a cold winter's night that was so deep.
        Nowell, nowell, nowell, nowell,
        Born is the King of Israel.

They looked up and saw a star
Shining in the east, beyond them far,
And to the earth it gave great light,
And so it continued both day and night.
        Nowell, nowell, nowell, nowell,
        Born is the King of Israel.

And by the light of that same star,
Three wise men came from country far;
To seek for a King was their intent,
And to follow the star wherever it went.
        Nowell, nowell, nowell, nowell,
        Born is the King of Israel.

This star drew nigh to the north-west,
O'er Bethlehem it took its rest,
And there it did both stop and stay
Right over the place where Jesus lay.

Nowell, nowell, nowell, nowell,
Born is the King of Israel.

Then did they know assuredly,
Within that house the King did lie;
One entered in then for to see,
And found the Babe in poverty.
Nowell, nowell, nowell, nowell,
Born is the King of Israel.

Then enter'd in those wise men three,
Most reverently upon their knee,
And offer'd there, in His presence,
Both gold, and myrrh, and frankincense.
Nowell, nowell, nowell, nowell,
Born is the King of Israel.

Between an ox-stall and an ass,
This child truly there born He was;
For want of clothing they did Him lay
All in the manger, among the hay.
Nowell, nowell, nowell, nowell,
Born is the King of Israel.

Then let us all, with one accord,
Sing praises to our Heavenly Lord,
That hath made heaven and earth of nought
And with His blood mankind hath bought.
Nowell, nowell, nowell, nowell,
Born is the King of Israel.

If we in our time shall do well,
We shall be free from death and hell;

For God hath prepared for us all
A resting-place in general.
Nowell, nowell, nowell, nowell,
Born is the King of Israel.

One by one they each chose a carol, and struck up the tunes. All the children knew the words well – even Ann – for they had them at school, and had learnt them properly. It was a very Christmassy evening.

When everyone had chosen his or her carol there was a silence. Then suddenly there came a loud knock at the door, and a voice cried, 'The mummers are here!'

'Well!' said Daddy, getting up, 'it's a long time since any mummers came! Shall we let them in and see them do their play? It will be rather amusing, I expect.'

In excitement the children crowded to the front door, whilst Daddy asked the mummers in. They were children from the village, all dressed up.

'Come into the big lounge and do your mumming there,' said Daddy, and the children trooped in, giggling. They began their play. Here it is.

THE MUMMER'S PLAY*

(*Enter the Presenter*)

Presenter.   I open the door, I enter in;
I hope your favour we shall win.
Stir up the fire and strike a light,
And see my merry boys act tonight.
Whether we stand or whether we fall,
We'll do our best to please you all.
(*Enter the actors, and stand in a clump*)

* From *The English Folk Play*. Edited by Sir E. K. Chambers. By kind permission of the Clarendon Press.

Presenter.   Room, room, brave gallants all,
    Pray give us room to rhyme;
    We're come to show activity,
      This merry Christmas-time;
    Activity of youth,
    Activity of age,
    The like was never seen
      Upon a common stage.
    And if you don't believe what I say,
    Step in St George – and clear the way.
                   (*Enter St George*)

St George.   In come I, St George,
  The man of courage bold;
With my broad axe and sword
  I won a crown of gold.
I fought the fiery dragon,
  And drove him to the slaughter,
And by these means I won
  The King of Egypt's daughter.
Show me the man that bids me stand;
I'll cut him down with my courageous hand.
                (*Enter Bold Slasher*)

Presenter.   Step in, Bold Slasher.

Slasher.   In come I, the Turkish Knight,
    Come from the Turkish land to fight.
  I come to fight St George,
    The man of courage bold;
  And if his blood be hot,
    I soon will make it cold.

St George. Stand off, stand off, Bold Slasher,
  And let no more be said,
 For if I draw my sword,
  I'm sure to break thy head.
 Thou speakest very bold,
  To such a man as I;
 I'll cut thee into eyelet holes,
  And make thy buttons fly.

Slasher. My head is made of iron,
  My body is made of steel,
 My arms and legs of beaten brass;
  No man can make me feel.

St George. Then draw thy sword and fight,
  Or draw thy purse and pay;
 For satisfaction I must have,
  Before I go away.

Slasher. No satisfaction shalt thou have,
 But I will bring thee to thy grave.

St George. Battle to battle with thee I call,
 To see who on this ground shall fall.

Slasher. Battle to battle with thee I pray,
 To see who on this ground shall lay.

St George. Then guard thy body and mind thy head,
 Or else my sword shall strike thee dead.

Slasher. One shall die and the other shall live;
 This is the challenge that I do give.
      (They fight. Slasher falls)

The children all clapped loudly when the queer little play was finished, and the Slasher had fallen heavily to the ground with a most realistic groan.

'That was fine!' cried Ann. 'I wish you could do it all over again!'

'No,' said Mother, firmly. 'There isn't time. Look, here is some cocoa and biscuits for the mummers. We will share it with them.'

The mummers gulped down their cocoa, ate their biscuits, said their thanks and went off to do their mumming play to the neighbours. Mother looked at the clock.

'It's getting a bit late,' she said.

'Well, we're not going to bed without our Christmas story,' said Peter, at once. 'Mother, you wouldn't break *our* old custom, would you? You've told us the Christmas story now every Christmas Eve without a stop. I don't remember a Christmas Eve when we haven't all been sitting cosily round the fire like this, listening to you.'

'Well, you shall once again,' said his mother, smiling round at the family, whose faces were all glowing in the light of the burning Yule log. 'It's a story you all know well, and have heard many many times, but everyone should hear it or read it again at Christmas-time, because it is such a beautiful tale.'

'We're ready,' said Peter, slipping down on to the hearth-rug. 'Begin, Mother.'

So Mother began the old story, in her low, clear voice, and all the family listened.

The Christmas Story

Now when Joseph and Mary
Were to Bethlehem bound,
They with travelling were weary,
Yet no lodging they found
In the City of David,
Though they sought o'er all;
They alas could not have it,
But in an ox's stall.

THE FIRST CHRISTMAS

Nearly two thousand years ago there lived in the town of Nazareth in Palestine a girl called Mary. One day an angel came to her with great news.

'Hail, Mary!' said the angel. 'I bring you great tidings. You will have a little baby boy, and you must call him Jesus. He shall be great, and shall be called the Son of the Highest. He will be the Son of God, and of his kingdom there shall be no end.'

Now Mary was only a little village girl, and she could hardly believe this news; but as she gazed up at the angel, she knew that it was true. She was full of joy and wonder. She was to have a baby boy of her own, and He was to be the little Son of God.

Mary married a carpenter called Joseph, and together they lived in a little house on the hillside. She could hear him hammering at his work, as she went about the little house.

Her heart sang as she thought of the tiny baby who was to come to her that winter.

The summer went by, and it was autumn. Then the winter came – and with it arrived men who put up a big notice in the town. Mary went to read it.

It was a notice saying that everyone must go to their own home-town and pay taxes. This meant that Mary and Joseph must leave Nazareth, and go to Bethlehem, for that was where their families had once lived.

Mary did not feel very strong just then, and the thought of the long walk to Bethlehem filled her with dismay. But Joseph comforted her.

'You shall ride on the donkey,' he said. 'I will walk beside you. We shall be three or four days on the way, but the little donkey will take you easily.'

So Mary and Joseph set off to go to Bethlehem. Mary rode on the little donkey, and Joseph walked beside her, leading it. Many other people were on the roads too, for everyone had to go to pay their taxes. Mary and Joseph travelled for some days, and one night Mary felt tired.

'When shall we be there?' said Mary. 'I feel tired. I want to lie down and rest.'

'There are the lights of Bethlehem,' said Joseph, pointing through the darkness to where some lights twinkled on a hilltop. 'We shall soon be there.'

'Shall we find room at Bethlehem?' said Mary. 'There are so many people going there.'

'We will go to an inn,' said Joseph. 'There you will find warmth and food, comfort and rest. We shall soon be there.'

When they had climbed up the hill to the town of

Mary rode on the little donkey, and Joseph walked beside her, leading it

Bethlehem, Mary felt so tired that she longed to go to the inn at once.

'Here it is,' said Joseph, and he stopped the little donkey before a building that was well lighted, and from which came the sounds of voices and laughter. Then Joseph called for the inn-keeper, and a man came to the door, holding up a lantern so that he might see the travellers.

'Can you give us a room quickly?' said Joseph. 'My wife is very tired, and needs to rest at once.'

'My inn is full, and there is not a bed to be had in the whole town. People have been coming here all day long,' said the inn-keeper. 'You will find nowhere to sleep. There is no room at the inn.'

'Can't you find us a resting-place somewhere?' said Joseph, anxiously. 'My wife has come so far and is so tired.'

The man swung his lantern up to look at Mary, who sat patiently on the donkey, waiting. He saw how tired she was, how white her face looked, and how patiently she sat there. He was filled with pity, and he wondered what he could do.

'I have a cave at the back of my inn, where my oxen sleep,' he said. 'Your wife could lie there. I will have it swept for you, and new straw put down. But that is the best I can offer you.'

'Let me lie in the stable, Joseph,' said Mary. 'I cannot go any farther now.'

So Joseph said they would sleep in the cave that night. Whilst a servant swept out the stall where they were to lie, he helped Mary off the donkey. She walked wearily round to the cave in the hillside, and saw the servant putting down piles of clean straw for her. From nearby stalls big-eyed oxen stared

Mary lay down in the straw

round, munching, wondering who had come to share their stable that night. Doves on the rafters took their heads from under their wings, and watched with bright eyes.

Mary lay down in the straw. Joseph looked after her tenderly. He brought her milk to drink, he made her a pillow from a rug, and he hung his cloak over the doorway so that the wind could be kept away.

Their little donkey was with them in the stable too. He ate his supper hungrily, looking round at Mary and Joseph as he munched. Mary smelt the oxen, and felt the warmth their bodies made. She saw their breath steaming in the light of the lantern hung from a nail.

And that night Jesus was born to Mary, in the little stable

at Bethlehem. Mary held him closely in her arms, looking at Him with joy and love. The oxen looked round too, and the little donkey stared with large eyes. The doves watched and cooed softly. The little Son of God was there!

'Joseph, bring me the clothes I had with me,' said Mary. 'I thought perhaps the Baby would be born whilst we travelled, and I brought His swaddling-clothes with me.'

In those far-off days the first clothes a baby wore were called swaddling-clothes. He was wrapped round and round in a long piece of linen cloth. Mary took the linen from Joseph, and wrapped the Baby in His swaddling-clothes. Then she wondered where to put Him, for she wanted to sleep.

'He cannot lie on this straw,' said Mary, anxiously. 'Oh, Joseph, we have no cradle for our little Baby.'

'See,' said Joseph, 'there is a manger here full of soft hay. It will be a cradle for Him.'

Joseph put the tiny Child into the manger, laying Him down carefully in the soft hay. How small He was! How downy His hair was, and how tiny His fingers were with their pink nails!

Then Mary, tired out, fell asleep on the straw, whilst Joseph kept watch beside her, and the Baby slept peacefully in the manger nearby. The lantern light flickered when the wind stole in, and sometimes the oxen stamped on the floor.

That was the first Christmas, the birthday of the little Christ-child. The little Son of God was born, the great teacher of the world – but only Joseph and Mary knew that at last He had come.

No bells rang out at His birth. The people in the inn slept soundly, not guessing that the Son of God was in a nearby stall. Not one person in the town of Bethlehem knew the great news that night.

But the angels in heaven knew the great happening. They must spread the news. They must come to our world and tell someone. They had kept watch over the city of Bethlehem that night, and they were filled with joy to know that the little Son of God was born.

THE SHEPHERDS ON THE HILLSIDE

Then God sent an angel from heaven so high
To certain poor shepherds in fields where they lie.

Who was awake to hear the angels' news? There was no one in the town awake that night, but on the hillside outside Bethlehem there were some shepherds, watching their sheep.

Good shepherds always watched their sheep at night, in case wolves came to steal the lambs. They took it in turn to watch, and that night, as usual, there was a company of shepherds together, wrapped in their warm cloaks, keeping guard over their flocks.

They talked quietly together. They had much to talk about that night, for they had watched hundreds of people walking and riding by their quiet fields, on the way to pay their taxes at Bethlehem. It was seldom that the shepherds saw so many people.

As the shepherds talked, looking round at their quiet sheep, a very strange thing happened. The sky became bright, and a great light appeared in it, and shone all round them. The shepherds were surprised and frightened. What was this brilliant light that shone in the darkness of the night?

They looked up fearfully. Then in the middle of the dazzling light they saw a beautiful angel. He shone too, and he spoke to them in a voice that sounded like mighty music.

'See,' said one shepherd to another in wonder. 'An angel.'

They all fell upon their knees, and some covered their faces with their cloaks, afraid of the dazzling light. They were trembling.

Then the voice of the angel came upon the hillside, full of joy and happiness.

'Fear not; for, behold, I bring you good tidings of great joy, which shall be to all people. For unto you is born this day in the City of David a Saviour, which is Christ the Lord. And this shall be a sign unto you; ye shall find the Babe wrapped in swaddling-clothes, lying in a manger.'

The shepherds listened in the greatest wonder. They were simple countrymen, and it was hard for them to understand what was happening, and what the angel meant. The Son of God was born in Bethlehem – not far from them? How could that be?

They gazed at the angel in awe, and listened to this wonderful being with his great, overshadowing wings. As they looked, another strange thing happened, which made the shepherds tremble even more.

The dark sky disappeared, and in its place came a crowd of shining beings, bright as the sun, filling the whole sky. Everywhere the shepherds looked there were angels, singing joyfully.

'Glory to God in the highest,' sang the host of angels, 'and on earth peace, goodwill towards men. Glory to God in the highest, and on earth peace, goodwill towards men.'

Over and over again the angels' voices sang these words, and the shepherds, amazed, afraid and wondering, listened and marvelled. They had never before imagined such a host of shining angels, never before heard on their quiet hillside such a wonderful song. Surely all the angels in heaven were over Bethlehem that night.

Then, as the shepherds watched, the dazzling light slowly faded away, and the darkness of the night came back. The angels vanished with the light, and at last all that could be heard was a faint echo of their voices, still singing 'Glory to God in the highest'.

And then the sky was quite dark again, set with twinkling stars that had been out-shone by the glory of the angels. A sheep bleated and a dog barked. There was nothing to show that heaven had opened to the shepherds that night.

The frightened men were silent for a time, and then they began to talk in low voices that gradually became louder.

'They were angels. How dazzling they were. We saw angels. They came to us, the shepherds on the hillside.'

'It couldn't have been a dream. Nobody could dream like that.'

'I was frightened. I hardly dared to look at the angels at first.'

'Why did they come to us? Why should they choose men like us to sing to?'

'You heard what the first angel said – he said a Saviour had been born to us, Christ the Lord. He said that he was born in the City of David tonight – that means in Bethlehem, for Bethlehem is the City of David!'

'Can it be true?'

'Why should all the angels of heaven come and tell us this? Are we the only ones awake in Bethlehem? Oh, what wonderful news this is. I can hear the angels' song in my head still.'

'We will go and find the little King. I want to see Him.'

'We cannot go at midnight. And how do we know where He is?'

'We *must* go! Why should the angels have come to tell us this news, and even told us that the Babe is wrapped in swaddling-clothes lying in a manger, if they had not meant us to go and worship Him?'

'Why should the Holy Child be put in a manger? Surely He should have a cradle!'

'He must have been born to one of the late travellers, who could find no room at the inn. They must have had to put Him in a manger. I am going to see.'

The shepherds, excited and full of great wonder, went up the hillside to Bethlehem. They left all their dogs to guard the sheep, except for one who went with them.

Soon they came to the inn, and, at the back, where the stable was built into the hillside cave, they saw a light. 'Let us go to the stable and see if the Son of God is there,' whispered one shepherd. So, treading softly, they went round to the back of the inn, and came to the entrance of the stable. Across it was stretched Joseph's rough cloak to keep out the wind. The shepherds peered over it into the stable.

They saw what the angel had told them – a Babe wrapped in swaddling-clothes, lying in a manger!

On the straw, asleep, was Mary. Nearby was Joseph, keeping watch over her and the Child.

'There's the Baby,' whispered the shepherds, in excitement.

'In the manger, wrapped in swaddling-clothes. There is the Saviour, the little Son of God.'

Joseph and Mary heard the low voices, and Joseph went to see who was outside the entrance. 'What do you want?' he asked.

Then the shepherds told Joseph about the great light in the sky, and the singing angels. They told him that the first bright angel had said they would find the Babe lying in a manger, so they had come to find Him.

Mary heard what they said. She lifted the Child from the manger and took him on her knee. The shepherds knelt down before Him and worshipped Him. Again and again they told the wondering Mary all that had happened. She held her Child close, and marvelled at what she heard. Angels had come to proclaim the birth of her tiny Son!

The oxen stared, and the dog pressed close to his master, wondering at the strange happenings of the night. Then, seeing that Mary was looking tired, the shepherds went at last, walking softly in the night.

'We will tell everyone the news tomorrow!' said the shepherds. 'Everyone! What will they say when they know that whilst they slept we have seen angels?'

'What was the song the angels sang?' said one. 'And what did the first angel say?'

'He said "Fear not, for behold I bring you good tidings of great joy",' said another. 'And the others sang "Glory to God in the highest . . ." '

Down the hill they went, back to their sheep, sometimes looking up into the sky to see if an angel might once again appear. All through that night they talked eagerly of the angels, the Holy Child in the stable, and of Mary, His gentle mother.

The next day they told everyone of what had happened to them in the night, and many people went to peep in at the stable, to see the little Child.

Mary held Him close to her, and thought often of the angel she herself had seen some months before. She thought of the excited shepherds, and the host of shining angels they too had seen and heard. Her Baby was the little Son of God. Mary could hardly believe such a thing was true.

THE THREE WISE MEN

And by the light of that same star
Three wise men came from country far.
To seek for a King was their intent.
And to follow the star wherever it went.

Far far away from Bethlehem in a land that lay to the east, there lived some wise and learned men. At night these men studied the stars in the heavens. They said that the stars showed them the great thoughts of God. They said that when a new star appeared, it was God's way of telling men that some great thing was happening in the world.

Then, one night, a new star appeared in the sky, when the wise men were watching. The second night the star was brighter still. The third night it was so dazzling that its light seemed to put out the twinkling of the other stars.

'God has sent this star to say that something wonderful is happening,' said the wise men. 'We will look in our old, old books, where wisdom is kept, and we will find out what this star means.'

So they studied their old wise books, and they found in them a tale of a great King who was to be born into the world to rule over it. He was to be King of the Jews, and ruler of the world.

'The star seems to stand over Israel, the kingdom of the Jews,' said one wise man. 'This star must mean that the great King is born at last. We will go to worship Him, for our books say He will be the greatest King in the world.'

'We will take him presents of gold and frankincense and myrrh,' said another. 'We will tell our servants to make ready to go with us.'

So, a little while later, when the star was still brilliant every night in the sky, the three wise men set off on their camels. They were like kings in their own country, and a great train of servants followed behind on swift-footed camels. They travelled for many days and nights, and always at night the great star shone before them to guide them on their way.

They came at last to the land of Israel, where the little Jesus had been born. They went, of course, to the city where the Jewish king lived, thinking that surely the new little King would be there, in the palace at Jerusalem.

Herod was the king there, and he was a wicked man. When his servants came running to tell him that three rich men, seated on magnificent camels, with a train of servants behind them, were at the gates of the palace, Herod bade his servants bring them before him.

The wise men went to see Herod. They looked strange and most magnificent in their turbans and flowing robes. They asked Herod a question that amazed and angered him.

'Where is the child who is born King of the Jews?' they said. 'His star has gone before us in the east, and we have brought presents for Him, and we wish to worship Him. Where is He?'

'*I* am the king,' said Herod, full of anger. 'What is this child you talk of? And what is this star?'

The wise men told him all they knew. 'We are certain that a great King has been born,' they said, 'and we must find Him. Can you not tell us where He is?'

Herod sat silent for a moment. Who was this new-born King these rich strangers spoke of? Herod did not for a moment disbelieve them. He could see that these men were learned, and knew far more than he did.

'I will find out where this new-born King is, and kill Him,' thought Herod to himself. 'But this I will not tell these men. They shall go to find the Child for me, and tell me where He is – then I will send my soldiers to kill Him.'

So Herod spoke craftily to the wise men. 'I will find out what you want to know. I have wise men in my court who know the sayings of long-ago Jews, who said that in due time a great King would be born. Perhaps this is the Child you mean.'

Then Herod sent for his own wise men and bade them look in the books they had to see what was said of a great King to be born to the Jews. The learned men looked and they found what they wanted to know.

'The King will be born in the city of Bethlehem,' they said.

'Where is that?' asked the wise men.

'Not far away,' said Herod. 'It will not take you long to get there.'

'We will go now,' said the three wise men, and they turned to go. But Herod stopped them.

'Wait,' he said, 'when you find this new-born King, come back here to tell me where He is, for I too would worship Him.'

The wise men did not know that Herod meant to kill the little King, and not to worship Him. 'You shall be told where He is,' they said. 'We will return here and tell you.'

Then they mounted their camels and went to find the city of Bethlehem, which, as Herod had said, was not far away.

The sun set, and once again the brilliant star flashed into the sky. It seemed to stand exactly over the town of Bethlehem. The strangers, with their train of servants, went up the hill to Bethlehem, their harness jingling, and their jewelled turbans and cloaks flashed in the brilliant light of the great star.

They passed the wondering shepherds, and went into the little city. They stopped to ask a woman to guide them.

'Can you tell us where to find a new-born child?' they asked.

The woman stared at these rich strangers in surprise. She felt sure they must want to know where Jesus was, for everyone knew how angels had come to proclaim His birth.

'Yes,' she said, 'you will find the Baby in the house yonder. He was born in the stable of the inn, because there was no room for Him – but now that the travellers have left the city, room was found for His parents at that house. You will find Him there with His mother.'

The star seemed to stand right over the house to which the woman pointed. The wise men felt sure it was the right one. They made their way to it.

When Mary saw these three magnificent men kneeling before her tiny Baby, she was amazed. Angels had come to proclaim His birth, shepherds had worshipped Him – and now here were three great men kneeling before Him.

'We have found the little King,' said one wise man. 'We

have brought Him kingly presents. Here is gold for Him, a gift for a King.'

'And here is sweet-smelling frankincense,' said another.

'And I bring Him myrrh, rare and precious,' said the third. These were indeed kingly gifts, and Mary looked at them in wonder, holding the Baby closely against her. He was her own Child, but He seemed to belong to many others too – to the angels in heaven, to the simple shepherds in the fields, to wise and rich men of far countries. He had been born for the whole world, not only for her.

The wise men left and went to stay for the night at the inn. There was room for them, because the travellers who had thronged the little city had left some time before.

'Tomorrow we will go back to Herod and tell him where the new-born King is, so that he may come and worship Him,' said the wise men. But in the night God sent dreams to them, to warn them not to return to Herod, but to go back to their country another way.

So they mounted their camels, and returned to their country without going near Jerusalem, where Herod lived.

In vain Herod waited for the three wise men to return. His servants soon found out that they had been to Bethlehem but had returned home another way. This made Herod so angry that he hardly knew what he was doing.

First he sent his soldiers after the wise men to stop them, but they were too far away. Then he made up his mind to find the new-born Baby and kill Him.

But no one knew where the Child was, nor did they even know how old He might be. The wise men themselves had not known how old the Baby was. Herod sat on his throne, his heart black and angry.

'Call my soldiers to me,' he said at last.

They came before him, and Herod gave them a cruel and terrible command.

'Go to the village of Bethlehem and kill every boy-child there who is under two years old,' he said. 'Go to the villages round about and kill the young baby boys there too. Let no one escape.'

The soldiers rode off, their harness jingling loudly. They rode up the hill to Bethlehem, and once again the quiet shepherds stared in wonder at strange visitors. But soon, alas, they heard the screams and cries of the mothers whose little sons had been killed, and they knew that something dreadful was happening.

Every boy-child was killed by the cruel soldiers, and when their terrible work was done, they rode down the hills again, past the watching shepherds, to tell Herod that his commands had been obeyed.

'There is no boy-child under two years old left in Bethlehem or the villages nearby,' said the captain of the soldiers, and Herod was well pleased.

'The new-born King is dead,' he thought. 'I have been clever. I have killed the Baby who might one day have been greater than I am.'

But Jesus was not killed. He was safe. On the night that the wise men had left Mary, the little family had gone to bed, and were asleep. But, as Joseph slept, an angel came to him in his dreams, and spoke to him.

'Arise,' said the shining angel. 'Take the young Child and His mother, and flee into Egypt, and stay there until I tell you to return; for Herod will seek the young Child to destroy Him.'

Joseph awoke at once. He sat up. The angel was gone, but the words he had said still sounded in Joseph's ears. Joseph knew that there was danger near, and he awoke Mary at once.

'We must make ready and go,' he said, and he told her what the angel had said. Then Mary knew they must go, and she went to put her few things into a bundle, and to lift up the Baby Jesus. Joseph went to get the little donkey, and soon, in the silence of the night, the four of them fled away secretly.

They went as quickly as they could, longing to pass over into the land of Egypt, which did not belong to Herod. He would have no power over them there.

So, when Herod's soldiers came a little later to the city of Bethlehem, Jesus was not there. He was safe in Egypt, where Herod could not reach Him.

And there, until it was safe for Him to return to His own country, the little new-born King lived and grew strong, and kind and loving. No one knew He was a King. His father was a carpenter, and His friends were the boys of the villages around.

But His Mother knew. Often she remembered the tale of the shepherds who had seen the angels in the sky, and she remembered too the three wise men who had come to kneel before her Baby. She still had the wonderful presents they had given to her for Him. He would one day be the greatest King in the world.

But it was not by power or riches or might that the Baby in the stable grew to be the greatest man the world has ever seen. It was by something greater than all these – by LOVE alone.

That is the story of the first Christmas, which we remember to this day, and which we keep with joy and delight.

There was a silence after Mother had finished telling the story

There was a silence after Mother had finished telling the story. Nobody spoke for quite a minute. The Yule log sent up a shower of sparks, and the children watched them. Then Ann gave a deep sigh.

'Thank you, Mother. You do tell the Christmas story well – you make it so real. You make me feel as if I want to be one of the shepherds peering into the stable – or even one of the wise men's servants peering over his master's shoulder just to get a glimpse of the little Jesus.'

'It *is* a wonderful old story,' said Benny, his eyes shining. 'I don't mind how many times I hear it, when it is told like you tell it, Mother. I wish I had been on the hillside with the shepherds.'

'It will soon be the Christ-child's birthday,' said Susan.

'It's nice to think that although we can't give *Him* presents, we can give other people gifts instead. We keep His birthday that way.'

The clock struck, and Ann and Peter frowned at it. It always struck just at the wrong time and reminded Mother that it was getting late.

It reminded her now. 'Time for your supper,' she said. 'Then you must hang up your stockings and go to bed. Otherwise you will certainly not be asleep when Santa Claus comes.'

'Oh, Mother – would you tell us the story of Santa Claus himself, before we go?' begged Peter.

'Certainly not,' said Mother. 'To begin with there's no more time left, and to end with, I don't know anything about him, I'm afraid.'

'Do you, Daddy?' asked Susan. Her father shook his head.

'Well no, I don't,' he said. 'I don't even know how he got his name, or why he comes, or anything. Anyway, I really think you know enough about Christmas-time now. Come and have your suppers.'

They all sat down at the table. They were hungry. Ann and Peter were very sleepy, for it was long past their usual bed-time.

'Now, upstairs all of you,' said Mother. 'And I'm sure I need hardly remind you – hang your stockings up!'

A Visitor in the Night

'Twas the night before Christmas, when all through the house,
Not a creature was stirring, not even a mouse,
The stockings were hung by the chimney with care
In the hope that St Nicholas soon would be there.

Clement Moore

'I'm going to hang up my longest stocking,' said Susan, and she took out a very long one indeed, with no holes in it.

'I've borrowed one of Daddy's,' said Ann. 'My socks are too small.'

Peter and Benny hung up football stockings. 'Quite a collection of stockings for Santa Claus to fill,' said Benny.

'I know you don't believe in Santa Claus, but I do,' said Ann, getting into bed, and calling through the door to Benny. 'I'm going to wait up and ask him about himself. I want to know *his* story too. He must have got one!'

'You'll never keep awake!' said Susan, jumping into her bed.

'Here's Mother to say goodnight,' said Ann. 'Mother, who first thought of hanging up Christmas stockings? It's such a good idea!'

'I don't know,' said Mother. 'I only know that French and Dutch children used to put out their wooden shoes – their sabots – on Christmas Eve for presents to be put into them. So I suppose hanging up stockings came from much the same idea. Now – no more Christmas questions, Ann. Go to sleep, and wake up in the morning to find your stocking full from top to toe. But no getting out of bed until seven o'clock!'

Mother said goodnight to everyone, and turned out the lights. Benny and Peter fell asleep at once. Susan gave the little twitches she always did when she was almost asleep. She didn't answer when Ann spoke to her.

'Susan. Are you asleep?'

Ann lay quietly in her bed. It was quite dark. She didn't feel at all sleepy. She lay and wondered about Santa Claus. Who was he really? Why did he come secretly at Christmastime? Why didn't he like people to see him?

'I wish I *could* stay awake and see Santa Claus,' she thought. 'I don't feel a bit sleepy. But I suppose I ought to go to sleep. I'll try.'

She tried very hard. She screwed up her eyes, but they soon opened again, and looked into the darkness. She could hear Susan's steady breathing in the bed nearby.

'I'll make up a story in my mind,' thought Ann. 'That's a good way to make myself go to sleep.'

But she seemed wider awake than ever. Then she heard Daddy winding up the clock downstairs. That meant that he and Mummy were coming up to bed too. Goodness, it must be terribly late!

The clock in the hall struck loudly – just once. 'It's half past something,' said Ann. 'Half past ten or maybe half past eleven. I don't know which. Oh – here come Daddy and Mummy.'

She sat up as her mother came softly into the room, carrying a candle. She saw Ann looking at her and she was not very pleased.

'Ann! Not asleep yet? It's terribly late. Lie down at once.'

... *a soft scraping no*

Ann lay down with a sigh. Her mother and father went into their own room and Ann heard them talking in low voices. Then there was the creak of the bed. Daddy and Mother would soon be asleep. Ann would be the only one awake.

The grandfather clock downstairs ticked on through the night very loudly. Ann listened to him. He struck again – twelve times. So it was twelve o'clock. Midnight!

Ann turned over and shut her eyes again. Then she heard a noise in the distance that made her open her eyes with a jerk.

She heard bells. What a funny thing to hear in the middle of the night. They were not church bells – they were jingly bells, like the ones Ann and Peter had on their reins.

b on the roof . . .

Jingle-jingle-jingle, went the bells, coming nearer and nearer. Then there came a soft scraping noise up on the roof, and a low voice spoke. Ann couldn't hear what was said. The bells jingled once or twice more and then stopped.

Ann's heart beat very fast. She felt quite certain that Santa Claus had arrived. Those bells were the bells of his reindeer – that scraping noise was the sleigh landing on the roof. That low voice was the voice of Santa Claus himself.

The little girl slipped out of bed and went to the window to look out. She could only see the whiteness of the thick snow. As she looked out she heard a curious sound overhead.

'Exactly like a reindeer stamping a hoof on thick snow up on the roof,' thought Ann, her heart beating faster. 'Oh, I *know* it's Santa Claus. He's come. I wonder which chimney he'll come down.'

She thought for a moment. 'I think it will be the very big chimney we have in the lounge — the one we have been burning the Yule-log in tonight. I'll go down and hide myself and watch.'

The little girl put on her dressing-gown and slippers, for the night was very cold. She opened her bedroom door quietly and crept out into the passage. Down the stairs she went, as quietly as she could, and came at last to the half-open door of the lounge. The Yule log was still alight, so there was a glow from the fireplace.

No one was there — but what was that noise in the chimney? Ann's knees began to shake a little. It was all very well to keep awake like this and hope to see Santa Claus — but what would he say if he saw her? He might be very cross.

She hid behind the sofa and waited. The noise in the chimney went on — and then, to Ann's great excitement, a big pair of legs appeared down the great chimney-place of the hearth. They wore large-sized black boots. A grunting noise came down the chimney at the same time as the boots. Then, neatly avoiding the still-burning log, a stout red-clad body came down the chimney and landed on the hearth among the fire-irons. They made a little clatter.

Ann peeped above the sofa. Yes, it really and truly was Santa Claus. There was no mistake about it at all. He was dressed in red, and had a red hood over his head, edged with white fur. On his hands were enormous fur gloves. His face was red and plump and jolly, and his beard was as white as the snow outside.

Ann didn't feel a bit afraid of him when she saw his cheerful, jolly face. Santa Claus looked round the room, brushed his tunic with his hand, and sat down with a sigh on a chair by the fire.

'I'm getting too fat for chimneys,' Ann heard him say. Then he looked at the fire and gave the log a little kick with his boot, that made it flare up at once. The firelight flickered all over the room.

A jingling noise sounded, and Santa Claus got up at once and called softly up the chimney.

'Now then, Swift-One, stand still. You'll set the others fidgeting if you start!'

The jingling stopped. Santa Claus sat down again. Smoke blew out of the fireplace and he coughed. He looked round and gave an exclamation of annoyance.

He knelt down by the burning log, and thrust his great arm up the warm chimney. He pulled down a sack quite full of something.

'Toys,' thought Ann, her eyes shining. 'His sack of toys. What a nice, kind, generous old man he is. Oh, how I wish I could give *him* a present!'

Ann suddenly thought of a bottle of sweets she had. She had bought it with her own money, meaning to give it as a present to a friend, but then she had seen a handkerchief and she had bought that instead. So she had the bottle of sweets and no one to give it to – but she could give it to Santa Claus!

The sweets were in a nearby cupboard. Ann crawled to it and opened the door. She took out the sweets. Then trembling, stood up and spoke.

'Good evening, Santa Claus!'

Santa Claus gave an enormous jump and looked round, startled. He saw Ann, in her blue dressing-gown, standing near to him, looking rather scared.

'Bless us all!' he said, in a deep voice, 'what a fright you gave me.'

'Santa Claus, you're always giving other people presents, and now I've got one for *you*,' said Ann, and she held out the bottle of boiled sweets. Santa Claus took it and smiled.

'My favourite sweets – and plenty of red ones too – how lovely. Thank you, little girl – no one has ever given *me* a present before. Did you hear me come down the chimney?'

'Yes – and I heard the jingling of your reindeers' harness and bells,' said Ann. 'Oh Santa Claus, it's simply marvellous to see you. Are you real? I'm not dreaming, am I?'

'How am I to know if you're dreaming or not?' said Santa Claus.

'Well – my sister and brothers would know if I am dreaming,' said Ann, an idea coming into her head. 'Could I go and get them and let them see you? If they can see you, I shall know I'm not dreaming.'

'Fetch them, then,' said Santa Claus. 'Is that lemonade I see on the sideboard there? Could I have some, do you think? I feel very thirsty.'

'Oh Santa Claus – would you like some sandwiches, or biscuits – and some hot cocoa?' said Ann. 'Susan – that's my sister – can make lovely cocoa. We could all have some together, and talk to you. We'd like to ask you lots of questions.'

Santa Claus pulled out an enormous gold watch. 'Well,' he said, 'I've got a little time to spare – and hot cocoa and biscuits and a talk do sound rather nice. Go and fetch your sister and brothers, find out whether you are dreaming or not, and then let's have a cosy time together.'

Ann was so happy. She sped upstairs and into her own bedroom. She went to Susan and pulled her arm.

'Susan! Wake up. Quick, wake up. There's a visitor downstairs.'

Susan woke up. Ann had her torch on by now and Susan wondered what was happening. 'What is it?' she said. 'A visitor downstairs. You must be dreaming, Ann.'

'That's what I want to find out,' said Ann, 'because the visitor is Santa Claus, Susan. I thought perhaps I must be dreaming, so I came to get you and the boys – because then you can tell me if I am.'

Susan got up and put on her dressing-gown. She was puzzled and astonished, and quite excited. They went to get the boys, who were very hard to wake.

'Well, if Ann's dreaming, we all must be,' said Peter, not very pleased at being waked up so suddenly. 'What's all this about a visitor downstairs? Of course Ann is dreaming. There won't be anyone there when we get down.'

But there was. Santa Claus still sat there, huge and kindly, his face redder than ever by the light of the fire. The children stood still and stared at him.

'Golly – it *is* Santa Claus,' said Peter, and gave a squeal of delight.

'Sh!' said Susan. Ann caught her arm. 'Am I dreaming, Susan? Say I'm not! Say it's all real.'

'Well if you're dreaming, we *all* are,' said Susan.

'I don't see that it matters whether you are dreaming or not,' said Santa Claus, shaking hands with each of them. 'It's good, whatever it is, dream or reality. How do you do? It's so nice to get a welcome like this.'

'Well, we always thought that you didn't like being seen,' said Susan. 'Children are always told to be asleep when you come.'

'Ah, I come so late in the night, you see,' said Santa Claus.

'It wouldn't do for little children to lie awake for hours — they would be very tired on Christmas Day, and would get cross and naughty. Anyway, I prefer to do what I have to do quickly and secretly — though this does make a very nice change.'

'Susan, where are the biscuits?' said Ann, hopping about on one leg as she always did when she was excited. 'And can you make some cocoa? Santa Claus is thirsty.'

'Oh yes, of course I can,' said Susan, delighted. 'I'll bring a saucepan of milk in here.' She ran out and soon came back with a big saucepan of milk, a tin of cocoa, a tall jug, and a basin of sugar on a tray. She set the saucepan of milk on the fire to heat.

Benny had found the tin of biscuits and he took off the lid. Susan sent Ann to get five cups and saucers for the cocoa. Everyone felt happy and excited. This was a wonderful thing to happen in the middle of the night.

Soon the cocoa was made. Susan poured out five cups of the milky mixture, and added sugar. Then the biscuits were handed round, and everyone settled down to enjoy themselves and talk.

'Are your reindeer all right up on the cold roof?' said Ann, hearing a soft jingle just then.

'Oh yes,' said Santa Claus. 'I always throw a rug over each of them before I come down a chimney. How nice of you to think of them.'

'Santa Claus, we've often wondered who you really are,' said Peter shyly. 'How did you get your name? Is it really Claus? And what does Santa mean? And why do you come so secretly into people's houses? How was it you began to give presents?'

'What a list of questions!' said Santa Claus, sipping his

cocoa. 'I'd better tell you my own story, I think. Then you'll know all about me.'

'Oh *yes*,' said the children, together, and Benny poked the fire to make a good blaze.

'Well, to begin with, my name is not really Santa Claus,' said Santa Claus. 'My real name is Nicholas – Saint Nicholas.'

'How was it that you were called Santa Claus then?' said Ann, puzzled.

'I can tell you that,' said Santa Claus, taking another biscuit. 'The Dutch people have always called me 'San Nicolaas' which is Dutch for Saint Nicholas. Well, years and years ago, Dutchmen went to America, and there my name San Nicolaas was pronounced by the Americans as 'Santa Claus''. Say "San Nicolaas" quickly over and over again to yourselves and you will see how easily it becomes "Santa Claus".'

'San Nicolaas, San Nicolaas, Sanicolaas, Sanitclass, Santa Claus,' said the children, and saw for themselves exactly how the name Saint Nicholas or San Nicolaas became so easily the familiar one of Santa Claus.

'Yes, San Nicolaas, I see how you got your present name!' said Benny, pleased. 'I never knew that before.'

'Lots of words get changed through the years in that way,' said Santa Claus. 'I like my name of Santa Claus.'

'So do I,' said Ann. 'It suits you. Are you really a saint?'

'Yes,' said Santa Claus. 'Not that I feel like one, really. I don't believe saints do, you know. I was a bishop, away in Lycia, and I was tortured and put into prison because I believed in Jesus Christ, and His teaching. I always liked children. I was made a saint hundreds of years ago. People built a beautiful church for me in Bari – that's in Italy. Christians used to make pilgrimages there.'

'Saints help particular people, don't they?' said Benny. 'What kind of people do *you* specially help, Santa Claus – I mean, Saint Nicholas?'

'Well, I'm the patron saint of Russia,' said Santa Claus, drinking the last of his cocoa. 'And I'm the patron saint of travellers and sailors – and, of course, I'm the children's own saint too. I needn't tell you that.'

'No – we all know you belong to the children,' said Susan, and she poured Santa Claus out another cup of cocoa. 'Do you know, Santa Claus, our own church here is dedicated to you – it's called the Church of Saint Nicholas. Fancy, the church we go to on Sundays is the Church of Santa Claus!'

'Yes, I'm pleased to say I have about four hundred churches in your country,' said Santa Claus. 'My feast is held on December 6th. That is Saint Nicholas' Day.'

'So it is,' said Benny, remembering that he had seen it in his diary. 'I shall always think of you now on December 6th, Saint Nicholas!'

'You know, years ago, the churches used to elect a boy-bishop on my feast-day,' said Santa Claus. 'I used to like that. A boy was chosen from the choir to preside over the church as bishop until December 28th. He was dressed up in full bishop's robes with a mitre and a crozier, and he made a tour of the town. He blessed the people and he gave presents to all good children.'

'What a pity we don't choose boy-bishops now,' said Benny, thinking how much he would like to be one.

'Well, they do in one or two places,' said Santa Claus, 'but not nearly as often as they used to.'

'Tell us your story now, please,' said Ann. 'I do want to hear it.'

The Story of Santa Claus

He sprang to his sleigh, to his team gave a whistle,
And away they all flew like the down of a thistle.
But I heard him exclaim, ere they drove out of sight,
'Happy Christmas to all, and to all a goodnight!'

Clement Moore

Santa Claus looked into the fire for a moment or two, remembering old, old days. Then he began his story.

Long long ago, in the city of Myra in Lycia, there lived a poor man. He had three daughters growing up in his house, laughing and chattering just as you do.

The three girls used to talk of what they would do when they were married. Their father was so poor that they had few clothes, not enough to eat, and very few good times. It would be nice to marry, and have a home of their own, and husbands who could give them what they wanted.

'I shall have a fine house and a lovely garden,' said one.

'I shall have plenty of good food on my table and lovely clothes,' said another.

'I shall have beautiful children, and I shall ask our father to come and stay with me and be happy,' said the third.

So they talked of the happy time they hoped they would have when they were all grown up.

But, in those days, nobody wanted to marry girls without any money. Only those girls whose fathers could give them plenty of money were likely to make good marriages.

The father of the three girls was so poor that he could hardly have provided for one girl – and he had three. The poor man did not know what to do.

'I must try to marry them to good men, who will not ask for a great deal of money,' thought the father. So, when his daughters were grown up, he tried to find men who would marry them, and give them homes, without asking a great deal of money with each girl.

But alas, however much he tried, he could not find one man who would offer to marry one of his daughters. The time went on, and still the three girls lived in his poor home, feeling sad and miserable because there seemed no chance of having homes of their own.

'All our friends are married now,' they said to one another. 'Some have children to love. Only we are not married. It is a great disgrace. What is to happen to us?'

Their father grew so poor that he thought he would have to sell his daughters. The girls cried bitterly when they heard this. What a disgrace to be sold. What a miserable life they had to look forward to.

Now one day word was brought to me that these three girls were very unhappy. I knew them, and I was sorry for them. I could not bear to think that they would be sold, and would never know the happiness of a home and children of their own.

But I could not go to their father and offer him money. It would have to be done secretly. So, one night, when it was very dark, and no one could see me, I stole to this poor man's house. With me I had three purses full of money. There was one for each of the poor girls.

As I walked softly outside the house I could hear the girls

'I threw one purse after another over the high wall ...'

weeping. There was a high wall round the house, and I
thought I would throw the purses over it. Then, in the morning they would be found, and, as there were three, the girls
would guess that some secret friend had thrown them over
for their own use.

So I threw one purse after another over the high wall. I
heard them fall with a clank to the ground. Then I hurried
away in the night, my heart glad because I had been able to
save three people from a life of misery.

In the morning the girls looked out of the window and
they saw the three purses lying outside.

'What are those?' they wondered, and one went out to see.
She picked up the heavy purses, and they jingled with

money. She rushed indoors, crying loudly for joy, 'There is money here, much money!'

The girls opened the three purses and found the same amount of money in each one. 'There are *three* purses,' they said, 'and we are three girls. So one must be for each of us. Let us tell our father!'

Their father was overjoyed when he saw so much money. 'Now I shall not have to sell you,' he said. 'You can marry good men, and lead happy lives of your own.'

So the three girls were soon happily married, and went to good homes of their own. They never forgot the night when the money came over the wall, and I know they often spoke of it.

This secret giving of presents made me very happy. They did not know it was I who had given them the money, so they could not thank me, and I didn't want to be thanked. So, after that, I again and again gave presents in secret to those who needed my gifts.

And, even to this day, I do the same thing as you know. I come secretly to children, I give them presents without letting them see me do it, I creep away because I don't want any thanks. No one sees me – but tonight you have caught me, and here I am, telling you my story!'

The children had listened to Santa Claus telling his kindly tale, and had not made a movement. So that was how the custom began of giving presents secretly at Christmas-time. A kindly secret deed had made Saint Nicholas so happy, all those many years ago, that he had continued with his secret kindness, so that, to this very night, children all over the world hung up stockings for his secret gifts!

'How queer old customs are, with their histories reaching

so far back into the past,' said Susan. 'Our life isn't all in the present, is it, Santa Claus? It is made up of thousands of bits of the past, old things that happened, old names, old habits. The past and the present and the future all belong to one another.'

'Of course,' said Santa Claus. 'And we ought to live in them all, not just thoughtlessly in the present. We ought to know our past, and we ought to plan for our future. Then the present would always be worth living in.'

Ann thought the talk was getting rather solemn. She squeezed Santa Claus' hand.

'It was a lovely story,' she said, 'and it was just like you to do such a kind thing. I'd like to hug you for all your secret kindnesses, Santa Claus.'

'Well, I don't mind if you do,' said Santa Claus, beaming. So Ann hugged him, and he chuckled deep down in his beard.

'I always did like children,' he said. 'There's a lot more sense in them than in most grown-ups, and it's a pity you lose it as you grow. Well, well – I suppose I must be going.'

'No – don't go yet!' begged the children.

'My reindeer will be getting restive,' said Santa Claus. 'My sleigh and reindeer were an idea of the old Norsemen, you know, and a very good one, I think. My sleigh runs so lightly because, so the Norsemen said, it was built in Fairyland. It's easy to get about in it.'

'Why don't you give presents secretly on your own day, December 6th?' asked Peter.

'I used to,' said Santa Claus, 'but somehow people thought that Christmas was a better time for gifts, and I think it is myself. So I come on Christmas Eve, as you know, and you find my presents on Christmas Day – and other people's too, of course.'

'I suppose our Christmas festival began with the birthday of the Baby Jesus,' said Susan. 'Nearly two thousand years ago.'

'Oh, December 25th was a holiday or festival long long before that,' said Santa Claus. 'Many peoples held feasts at this time of year, even the Britains, before the birth of Christ. Then the early Christians took many of the old pagan ideas and customs, and used them in their own religion.'

'Does everyone now keep Christmas Day on December 25th?' asked Benny. 'Was it always kept on that day?'

'Oh no,' said Santa Claus. 'For some time, after Jesus Christ was born, the Church did not keep Christmas at all, and then later on the date was fixed for December 25th in the West, but January 6th in the East. It wasn't until a good many years had gone by that December 25th was celebrated by nearly everyone.'

'We have a cousin in Scotland,' said Ann, 'and do you know, she says that their great day there is not Christmas Day, but New Year's Day. Isn't that queer? Why is it?'

'Ah, I can tell you that,' said Santa Claus. 'About three hundred years ago, when Christmas was becoming rather a wild and unrestrained feast, many people were disgusted, and said that Christmas should be a sacred day, not a wild holiday. So Parliament forbade the keeping of Christmas Day as a feast or holiday. But it was not very long before the people were allowed once more to keep it as a real holiday. All but the Scottish people once again kept December 25th as a festival – but the Scots would not, and to this day they keep New Year's Day as their great holiday, and not Christmas Day.'

'I see,' said Peter. 'Now I know why Cousin Jeanie doesn't keep Christmas, but gets excited about New Year's Day. I never knew that before – and she didn't either, because I asked her. I'll write and tell her.'

'You won't know much about *this* Christmas Day, if I don't go soon!' said Santa Claus, getting up out of his chair.

'You'll all be so sleepy that you won't wake up until the afternoon – and you'll miss the pudding and everything!'

'We shall be awake all right!' said Susan, with a laugh. 'Are you really going, Santa Claus? It has been so lovely to hear your story and talk to you.'

'Just as nice for me,' said Santa Claus, beaming all over his ruddy, cheerful face. 'Listen to those reindeer of mine – getting quite impatient!'

The children could hear the stamping of hooves on the snow-covered roof, and the jingle of bells. Yes, it was time for Santa Claus to go!

'Now you hop upstairs as quickly as you can,' said Santa, pulling out his enormous watch again. 'Go along. You can watch out of the window for me, and see my sleigh going off.'

The children said goodnight, wished Santa Claus a happy Christmas, and went upstairs, pleased and happy. What a fine time they had had!

Ann pushed the bottle of sweets into his hand and gave him another hug when she said goodbye. She had quite lost her heart to the sturdy old man.

'I'm glad you're the children's saint,' she said. 'I'm glad to have a saint like you for my own. Goodnight!'

The four children watched at the window for Santa Claus to go. They saw and heard nothing for quite a while. 'I hope he hasn't got stuck in the chimney,' said Ann.

But, after some time, they heard the jingling of bells and harness, and off the roof slid the big sleigh, borne through the air as lightly as a feather. The moon shone out just then, and Santa Claus waved to the watching children at the window. Then he disappeared into the night, only a faint jingling coming on the air.

The children went back to bed. 'It hasn't been a dream, has it?' said Ann to Susan. 'Say it hasn't, Susan.'

'Well – I don't feel as if it has,' said Susan, 'but it really has been extraordinary, hasn't it? I'm very sleepy now. Goodnight, Ann.'

Christmas Day

So now is come our joyfullest feast;
Let every man be jolly.

George Wither

Ann awoke first on Christmas morning. The clock began to strike in the hall downstairs as she awoke. She counted the strokes – one, two, three, four, five, six, seven.

'Oh good,' said Ann, 'seven o'clock – and Christmas Day. I can look at my presents. But I forgot – of course Santa Claus didn't leave us any last night. He didn't come upstairs at all.'

She switched on the light, for it was still quite dark outside – and to her great amazement she saw that her stocking was quite full of toys. A lovely doll, with curly hair and a blue bow, peeped out of the top.

Susan's stocking was full too. How queer. Ann leaned over to Susan's bed and shook her.

'Susan! Wake up. Santa Claus has filled our stockings – but *when* did he do it?'

Susan awoke – and then there came the sound of voices and laughter from the boy's room.

'I say, you girls. Our stockings are full. Are yours? We'll bring ours in.'

There was the patter of feet, and Benny and Peter came in, carrying stockings that were almost bursting with toys.

'Look!' said Peter, pulling out a big top. 'Heaps of things.

Mother came into the room smilin

Now *when* did old Santa Claus come and fill our stockings?
That's what I would like to know. We were with him all the
time he was here. He couldn't possibly have slipped upstairs
without us seeing him.'

'*I* know when he filled them,' said Ann, suddenly. 'When
we were all watching and waiting for him at the window.
Don't you remember how we thought he was a very long
time – and I wondered if he had got stuck in the chimney?
That's when he came to fill them.'

'Of course!' said Benny. 'We were all pressing our noses to
the pane, and watching for him – and he was there behind
us, quietly stuffing toys into our stockings, in his usual
secret way – so we couldn't thank him.'

'Dear old Santa Claus,' said Ann. 'That's just like him. Look at this doll's chest-of-drawers in my stocking – isn't it sweet?'

Mother came into the room, smiling. 'I heard all the noise,' she said. 'Happy Christmas, dears!'

'Happy Christmas, Mother!' said the children, and kissed her. Then Ann told the great news.

'Mother – Santa Claus came in the night – and we all went down and saw him – and he told us his story, and lots of other things too.'

'You dreamt it,' said Mother, laughing.

'But Mother – we must *all* have dreamt the same dream then,' said Ann. 'We did have such a nice time. The Yule log was still burning – and we ate up all the biscuits.'

'What nonsense you talk,' said Mother. 'Now get back into bed, or you'll all catch cold.'

'Christmas Day at last,' said Peter, cuddling into Ann's bed to open his presents with Ann. 'It was such a long time coming – and it goes so quickly when it's here.'

'Christmas presents – and Christmas pudding – and a turkey – and crackers – and Christmas trees. What a lovely time it is,' said Ann, pulling a gorgeous pencil out of her stocking. 'Just look at this, Peter.'

'I'm jolly glad somebody began a festival at Christmas-time,' said Benny. 'It's one of the best old customs I know. I hope it will go on for ever.'

It was a lovely Christmas Day for the four children, and for the grown-ups too. The snow was still on the ground. The Yule log was actually still alight in the hearth and Mother broke off a bit to keep till the next Christmas, so that she might light the next log with it.

The pudding was brought in, all on fire, because Daddy had put brandy on it and then set light to it. 'Another old habit!' he said, 'and a most amusing one too. See how it burns.'

It was a delicious pudding. Ann had the silver thimble, and the other three had a sixpenny piece each, so that was lucky.

After tea the Christmas tree was lighted in the hall. How lovely it looked, as it stood there, its candles burning with a soft, glowing light. The ornaments glittered and swung, and the frost and tinfoil glistened like real frost and ice. The star at the top shone over the fairy doll, who looked down smil-ingly, just as she had done so many Christmasses.

'I love Christmas,' said Ann, dancing round the tree. 'And

I love it even more now I know such a lot about it. I wish somebody would write a book, and put into it all the things we know about Christmas-time.'

So I have – and here it is. And now we must leave Ann and her family with the lighted Christmas tree. The candles are almost burnt down. Christmas is nearly over.

But it will come again with all its love and kindliness, the birthday of the little Jesus born so many hundreds of years ago, and we will say once more, with the angels,

'GLORY TO GOD IN THE HIGHEST; AND ON EARTH PEACE,

GOODWILL TOWARDS MEN!'

Piccolo Book Selection

True Adventures and Picture Histories

Colour Books and Fiction

COLOUR BOOKS

Great new titles for boys and girls from eight to twelve. Fascinating full-colour pictures on every page. Intriguing, authentic easy-to-read facts.

DINOSAURS   Jane Werner Watson
SECRETS OF THE PAST
Eva Knox Evans
SCIENCE AND US
Bertha Morris Parker
INSIDE THE EARTH
Rose Wyler and Gerald Ames
EXPLORING OTHER WORLDS
Rose Wyler and Gerald Ames
STORMS   Paul E. Lehr
SNAKES AND OTHER REPTILES
George S. Fichter
AIRBORNE ANIMALS   George S. Fichter
25p each   Fit your pocket – Suit your purse

FICTION

For younger readers
ALBERT AND HENRY
Alison Jezard   20p
ALBERT IN SCOTLAND
Alison Jezard   20p

These and other PICCOLO Books are obtainable from all booksellers and newsagents. If you have any difficulty please send purchase price plus 7p postage to P.O. Box 11, Falmouth, Cornwall.
While every effort is made to keep prices low it is sometimes necessary to increase prices at short notice. PAN Books reserve the right to show new retail prices on covers which may differ from those advertised in the text or elsewhere.